edited by
Rhonda Bailey

Reading Nijinsky

By the same author

Suite pour un visage, Montréal, Éditions du Carré Saint-Louis, 1970.
Finitudes, Montréal, Éditions d'Orphée, 1972.
Yes, monsieur, Montréal, Éditions La Presse, 1973.
Un sens à ma vie, Montréal, Éditions La Presse, 1975.
J'elle, récit, Montréal, Éditions Stanké, 1979.
Une histoire gitane, Montréal, Québec/Amérique, 1982.
L'homme de Hong Kong, Montréal, Québec/Amérique, 1986.
Les miroirs d'Éléonore, Montréal, Éditions Lacombe (finalist for the Canada Council for the Arts Governor General's Literary Awards and for the Grand Prix littéraire du *Journal de Montréal*), 1989.
Chambre avec baignoire, Montréal, Québec/Amérique (Grand Prix littéraire du *Journal de Montréal* and Prix de la Société des écrivains canadiens), 1992; reprint: Montréal, XYZ éditeur, 2000.
Pense à mon rendez-vous, Montréal, Québec/Amérique (finalist for the Canada Council for the Arts Governor General's Literary Awards), 1994.
Traductrice de sentiments, Montréal, XYZ éditeur, "Romanichels" collection, 1995.
Le cimetière des éléphants, Montréal, XYZ éditeur, "Romanichels" collection, 1998.

Reading Nijinsky

a novel by **Hélène Rioux**

translated by
Jonathan Kaplansky

Originally published by XYZ éditeur as *Traductrice de sentiments*
Copyright © 1995 Hélène Rioux and XYZ éditeur
English translation © 2001 Jonathan Kaplansky and XYZ Publishing

All rights reserved. The use of any part of this publication reproduced, transmitted in any form or by any means, electronic, mechanical, photocopying, recording, or otherwise, or stored in a retrieval system without the prior written consent of the publisher – or, in the case of photocopying or other reprographic copying, a licence from Canadian Copyright Licensing Agency – is an infringement of the copyright law.

Canadian Cataloguing in Publication Data
Rioux, Hélène, 1949-
 [Traductrice de sentiments. English]
 Reading Nijinsky
 (Tidelines)
 Translation of: Traductrice de sentiments
 ISBN 0-9688166-5-7
 I. Kaplansky, Jonathan, 1960- . II. Title. III. Title: Traductrice de sentiments. English. IV. Series: Tidelines (Montréal, Quebec).

PS8585.I46T7313 2001   C843'.54   C2001-940957-5
PS9585.I46T7313 2001
PQ3919.2.R56T7313 2001

Legal Deposit: Fourth quarter 2001
National Library of Canada
Bibliothèque nationale du Québec

XYZ Publishing acknowledges the financial support our publishing program receives from the Canada Council for the Arts, the Book Publishing Industry Development Program (BPIDP) of the Department of Canadian Heritage, the ministère de la Culture et des Communications du Québec, and the Société de développement des entreprises culturelles.

Layout: Édiscript enr.
Cover design: Zirval Design
Cover photo: Yves Gauthier

Printed and bound in Canada

XYZ Publishing
1781 Saint Hubert Street
Montreal, Quebec   H2L 3Z1
Tel: (514) 525-2170
Fax: (514) 525-7537
E-mail: xyzed@mlink.net
Web site: www.xyzedit.com

Distributed by:
General Distribution Services
325 Humber College Boulevard
Toronto, Ontario   M9W 7C3
Tel: (416) 213-1919
Fax: (416) 213-1917
E-mail: cservice@genpub.com

*For my children,
in the hope that they never forget compassion...*
Hélène Rioux

*For Jessica Miller,
who opened a door
by encouraging me to translate.*
Jonathan Kaplansky

Tears start to come again between me and my view of the world.
>
> Mitia

I am a dancer.

I believe that we learn by practice. Whether it means to learn to dance by practicing dancing or to learn to live by practicing living, the principles are the same. In each it is the performance of a dedicated precise set of acts, physical or intellectual, from which comes shape of achievement, a sense of one's being, a satisfaction of spirit. One becomes in some area an athlete of God.

>
> Martha Graham, *Blood Memory*

Chapter 1

> She does not think of death, because she does not want to die. I think of death, because I do not want to die.
>
> Nijinsky, *Diary*

Mirabel. Dusk, the hour tinted with blue. Flashings in the fog. Crackling in the loudspeakers, unintelligible words, sepulchral voices. I look at my watch, but not impatiently. I have plenty of time.

A sudden rumbling. The plane begins to move, taxis to the end of the runway. With what seems to be inordinate effort, it takes flight, rising, flying over the dozing city, cutting through the clouds. Very calm, almost impassive, I sit near a window in the smoking section. In the seat next to me, a woman fumbles in her purse for a candy. She is wearing a burgundy suit and taupe-coloured hose. I don't like the colour burgundy. It evokes something crushed. Like raspberries trodden upon in the grass of an underbrush, a puddle of regurgitated wine, a black and blue mark, coagulated blood. Bruised taupe. Same shade as the lacquered nails of this passenger. Everything is bruised. I hear the sound of cellophane being unwrapped, out of the corner of my eye see a candy disappear into her mouth.

I am wearing blue jeans and a mohair sweater, soft and warm, with green and white stripes. My hands are empty. I don't feel like reading a book. My eyes are tired, my head saturated. I just want to close everything tightly, my eyes, my head, my heart. In the seat pocket in front of me a woman's magazine, so-called because of its advertisements for cosmetics, recipes, advice columns, fashion photos. I bought it at the newspaper stand in the airport. Simply turn the pages and a whole way of life jumps out at you. I will learn how to protect my skin from cancerous ultraviolet rays, how to behave with a hyperactive child, prepare an elegant brunch for two, six, or twelve guests. But I am going away alone. The cover, featuring an impeccably made-up pouting redhead, informs me that this special issue features the results of a survey on the sexual habits of forty-year-old women.

In five years I will be forty. This doesn't disturb me, but if they researched my sex life, I wonder what conclusions they would draw.

I look at my neighbour. She must be about forty, in the prime of life. If I asked her questions... And you, ma'am, how many lovers do you have? Do you have a preferred position? How many times a week? A month? Which method of contraception do you use? How many abortions? What kind of orgasm? Do you believe in love?

The emergency exits of the aircraft appear on the screens while a mellifluous male voice explains in Spanish and English how to inflate the life jackets should we fall into the middle of the Atlantic, how to use an oxygen mask in case of suffocation. An invisible flight attendant translates into incomprehensible French. I don't listen. I don't want to be saved if we fall into the ocean, or if we run out of oxygen. I don't want to be saved.

I check the contents of my purse. Passport, traveller's cheques, dark glasses, tube of frosted apricot lipstick, pen, toothbrush, mentholated cigarettes, lighter. Nothing in the luggage compartment. But at my feet, a red nylon bag in which I've packed a long cotton dress, three T-shirts, red, white, and black, tapes of Dead Can Dance and Bernard Lavilliers, my cleansing cream. Reduced to my simplest expression.

I forgot to mention the book. It's because of the book that I'm going abroad. I want to translate it, distance myself from everything. But I didn't forget. I simply didn't want to think about it. Not right now.

An insipid meal arrives on a tray. Stringy strips of pollock attempt to enliven anaemic-looking lettuce leaves next to an orange-coloured dressing in a plastic container: this is all meant to be, if I am to believe the menu, a crab salad. In a rectangular plate, a mediocre chicken in tomatoey hunter sauce, buttered carrots, and fragrant rice stagnate beneath a strip of tin foil. I am also entitled to a hard roll, stone-cold, and a triangle of *La Vache qui rit* cheese. Dessert is too pink to be real. I eat the cheese, drink the water and the wine. I wait.

A haughty-looking flight attendant circulates, teapot in hand. I hold out my cup, ask for lemon. Later, she removes my barely touched tray. My neighbour has devoured everything on hers.

In six hours, Madrid. The film is about to start. What is it? I look at the program: a comedy, it seems. Light. We will laugh. I feel heavy. I weigh at least three tons.

My neighbour is skimming through a glossy Iberia brochure. Images of a blue Mediterranean with sunny beaches, languid bodies. Yellow and red spots dot the blue: wind-surfers on the ocean. My neighbour is about to speak, I can sense it. The silence between us has gone on too long.

"Do you know Spain well?" she asks. I answer yes.

"I'm going to Marbella," she continues.

She informs me that she won a week-long trip by filling out an entry form in a branch of the liquor commission. She will stay in a five-star hotel frequented by movie stars and millionaires. Have use of the tennis courts, pools, sauna, workout facilities. A guided tour of the region is included, and a wine tasting.

"A trip for one? That's unusual."

"Two," she corrects.

Her friend was supposed to go with her, both of them were looking forward to it. But then, at the last minute, the day before yesterday, as it happened, he had a stupid accident, a fall on the ice in front of his house. He tore a ligament. She couldn't find anyone to take his place.

"Sometimes life plays rotten tricks," I say.

"What about you, are you also going on vacation?" she wants to know.

No, I'm going away for my work, a translation. I need peace. I'll find an apartment somewhere, in a small city in Andalusia near the sea. Off-season, it will be easy.

"A translation?"

"A book."

"A novel?"

I explain that I am a translator of what's called "the Love Collection."

"Oh..."

She knows it, has read a few titles. Not many, of course, but sometimes they're good to relax with after a hard day at work. She is a lab technician for a pharmaceutical company.

"On the beach, too, it's good," I remark.

She smiles. That's true, she brought a romance novel, *The Prisoner of Baghdad*. I tell her I translated that too. It was before the Gulf war, when Baghdad still conjured up images of *The Thousand and One Nights*. Her face lights up. She asks the title of what I'm translating now, so she can read it when it comes out. I tell her that I always come up with the title last.

"And you need peace to do the work?"

"I always need peace."

"A profession made in heaven. You're so lucky!"

"Always with love. Always on the wings of dreams."

"On the wings of dreams. It could be a title. If I saw it in a bookstore, I'd buy it without hesitating. On the wings of dreams."

"I'd buy it too," I tell her.

"My name is Claudine."

"I'm Éléonore."

"A name out of a novel."

"Claudine too."

The comedy has begun. But no one in the plane is laughing.

"Let's have a drink," she suggests. "After all, I won a trip to Spain. A reason to celebrate. I bought a bottle of gin at the duty-free."

We get up to fetch glasses, soda water, and ice at the flight attendant's station.

"To Spain!" I say, raising my glass.

"I'll drink, but my heart's not really in it... My friend and I had planned to rent a car and tour Portugal. In fact, we decided to stay three weeks. The flight and first week were paid for. Afterwards, we'd have stayed in pensions. We wanted to see everything. And now I'm here alone..."

"There are other fish in the sea."

"What?"

"I mean, you won't have trouble finding other men."

She protests, she's a faithful woman. She assures me that flings are a part of the past. With AIDS running rampant, mass murderers on the loose, all the psychopaths on the roads... Now love has become too dangerous. She doesn't want to end up disfigured, mutilated, hacked up. Or catch a terrible disease.

"The Spanish – how are they with women?" she asks.

"Spanish."

She laughs.

"But really?"

"You'll see."

We burst out laughing together, knowingly. We fill the glasses. We drink to Spain and the Spanish.

She brings up the name of Florent, whom she left in the hospital.

"It broke my heart to see him like that," she continues. "You know what cowards men are. And then, leaving him to go gallivanting around Spain while he... I felt... I don't know... I felt cruel. It ruins all my pleasure before I even get there. Perhaps I should have stayed. To provide moral support."

To get her mind off the subject, I tell her that my magazine features a survey on the sex lives of forty-year-old women. It might be fun to answer the questions.

"Question number one: is your sex life satisfactory?"

She hesitates.

"Well..."

"I'll answer first. My answer is no."

She gives a little laugh.

"Well, mine isn't either, not really. I mean, that's not all there is."

"Fortunately."

"As you say."

"But that *is* the subject of the survey."

"Come to think of it, yes."

"Yes what?"

"More or less satisfactory. Considering the circumstances."

"What do you mean by circumstances?"

"Being a forty-year-old woman."

"Extenuating."

"Yes?"

"The circumstances," I say.

"What do you think is extenuated?"

"Satisfaction, obviously."

"At forty, you expect less."

"Or require more. Question number two: do you have fantasies?"

"No."

"Question number three..."

"But you haven't answered the second!"

"Neither have you."

"Let's say that I have fantasies. Like everyone. But nothing really far-out. Normal ones. More like daydreams."

"The results of the survey show that 81 percent of women admit having fantasies. Often romantic. The Love Collection."

"Yes, that's sort of how it is for me too."

"They think of another man while making love."

"It can happen."

"The hero is strong and mysterious. Franz, Omar, Christopher. No Rogers or Maurices."

"No Florents either," she adds, laughing.

"This hero," I say, "has a square jaw, and thick hair. Unruly head of hair or locks that won't stay in place," I specify: "And to describe the way he looks at you?"

"Like steel," she answers without hesitation.

"Yes, like steel or like a wildcat. In any case, stress hard intensity. He certainly doesn't wear glasses."

"No, certainly not. Florent is farsighted. He wears them to read. What about his nose?"

"Aquiline, perhaps."

"I prefer straight."

"A straight nose is too ordinary."

"Maybe, but a really straight nose is quite rare. In any case, that's what I like."

"But a pug-nose or a ski slope, never."

"Perish the thought!" she exclaims.

"The haughty profile of a statue."

"I can see you have a way with words."

"Yes, I'm used to clichés," I say.

I continue:

"His voice could be described as vibrant and his smile sarcastic, sometimes even sardonic. A bitter smirk etched on his tanned face."
"With rugged features," she adds. "This man has suffered, life hasn't been easy for him."
"Betrayed by a young love."
"Ignominiously!"
"He became insensitive."
"Poor man!"
"He has broad shoulders," she continues. "An athletic build."
I add: "His muscles strain beneath the effort. Drops of sweat bead at his temples."
"Silver?"
"No, not silver, definitely not. Black as a raven's feathers, blond like a stalk of corn beneath the sun. Our hero does not age."
"A little more gin?"
"A drop. To keep the soda company."
She raises her glass: "To Franz! To Christopher!"
"When his shirt collar is open," I say, "you can see the hair on his chest."
"Virile."
"He drives a race car."
"Rides a horse."
"A thoroughbred."
"He owns an estate, a ranch."
"He lassoes animals beneath a burning sun."
"Or owns vineyards, factories, oil wells. In my dreams, he's always a rich, powerful man."
"Do you know that this is the first time I've ever had the opportunity of speaking with one of my readers?"
She defends herself: that's not all she reads. It's only when she's tired or restless. Otherwise she reads more serious works, literature, essays on the meaning of life. She suggests we call each other by the familiar *tu* instead of *vous*, now that we've opened up to each other. I offer

her a cigarette. We smoke in silence. Gin and cigarettes are good for the health, for mental health, that is. Because physical health... Cancer lies in wait for us, it seems, insidiously delving its tentacles into our organs. What a tragedy, this description of my poor charred lungs. They were pink at birth, what did I do to them? My soul was white, my heart pure, and my hymen intact, that's how I was. What did I do to everything given to me in good condition?

But I buy cigarettes low in tar and nicotine: it says so on the pack, along with the warning "cigarettes are addictive," which comforts me greatly.

The comedy unfolds on screen. I see images of a stairway, a man tearing down it, a woman screaming at a window, a suitcase landing on the sidewalk and opening, spilling open its contents of socks with holes and flowered boxer shorts to passers-by.

"In business, the hero is fair and pitiless," I say.

"In life, he is fearless," she adds.

"If he feels betrayed, he may go to a whorehouse or a sordid bar and drink himself into a stupor. He is a strong man with weaknesses."

"It's those weaknesses that make him so appealing," she concludes.

Each reader feels the instinct to train or reform awakening inside her, and each imagines that she will be the one to tame the beast. And at the same time, she nests, a dove at the throat of an eagle, desiring him while at the same time refusing him, pushing him away with frail arms; she wants him to force her, she wants to feel his strength, the brutal embrace. She wants the violence of waves crashing upon the shore, the fury of a hurricane uprooting trees. Every female reader is this woman. Women have the innate ability to train, convert. Their weapons: the sweetness and nobility of their feelings. Potentially, they are doves in love with predators. The same inescapable clichés have been repeated for centuries. The same seductions, the same balms on the same wounds.

"We were speaking of Florent," I say.

"Oh! Florent... well, to tell the truth, Florent has a flabby stomach, prudently drives a metallic grey Honda Civic and belongs to a bowling league. I also have a flabby stomach, cellulite, don't have a car, and go bowling with Florent on Saturday nights. Our lives are not spectacular, but I do love him, have learned to love him. We've been together six years. I read romance novels when I'm alone and sad. I enter contests to win trips. And when, for the first time in my life, I win one, I have to go away alone... I hope at least the weather will be good."

"The weather's always good. Almost always."

"At least if I can get some sun, it won't be a total loss. This is my only vacation this year. At the same time, it's funny, but I have the feeling that if I have a good time, I'll feel guilty."

"We always feel guilty, right? The next question?"

"First you have to talk about your own fantasies."

"The same ones, probably."

"Translating them, don't they become banal?"

"They're always banal."

I close my eyes for a moment.

"Sometimes the images are violent," I say.

"Violent?"

"I see myself dominated, bound, chained, subjugated."

"We're not responsible for images that come into our heads."

"They come, in spite of us. Although according to the survey, 7 percent of women admit indulging in this kind of fantasy."

"I wonder what percentage of men would admit to it... But personally, bound and defenceless, I'd be scared."

"I'd be scared too, in reality."

"Florent and I are very traditional when we make love."

"Men have a singular lack of initiative."

"In bed."

"Of course, in bed. With them it always has to happen in a bed."

"Yes, very comfortable," she concedes. "Afterwards they start snoring."

"Or else quickly get dressed to go home to their legitimate wife."

"Who's waiting in their bed."

"Personally," I say, "I like it outdoors. If I close my eyes I see a dark alley, a moon above."

"When you said outside, it wasn't an alley I'd imagined. My concept of a romantic fantasy is different. I'd choose a beach at sunset. Alone in the world. Lost in the universe."

"A beach, okay, but not alone in the world. I'd need people looking on."

"Oh, really – an exhibitionist?"

"We're talking about fantasy."

She fills our glasses.

"So let's drink to fantasy. Let's drink to phantoms."

"I'll continue," I say. "The beach at twilight. Our shapes are blurred, but our gestures defined. We undress each other standing up, face to face."

"Yes."

"No. The image isn't exciting enough. Too realistic."

"It was a good start, though."

"It's only a start."

Not long ago I lived with a man, but I wasn't in love. Philippe. I mean that our lives drifted apart, with no feeling of togetherness, in a quiet apartment, prettily decorated. I close my eyes to remember. Here's what comes to me: a tiny kitchen and his angular, bony body, his white chef's hat, his large apron. At the same time, aromas fill my memory: poached fish, white butter sauce. I remember chilly mornings, curled up in the big bed, him leaving for work, a tie, never the same, around his neck. Ties, his weakness. I made fun of his outdated elegance. Distinguished apparel, he corrected. When he came home, his briefcase would be overflowing with files. Urgent, as he'd say. Urgent, darling, my love. Swamped. Completely insane this week. And you, my love, did you have a good day? Me?

He was one of those people who mutter *Israeli-Arab conflict*, or *inflation, price wars, corruption*, sighing heavily, sadly nodding their heads. The weight of the world lay on his shoulders, immensely heavy. Sometimes he stooped. "Everything is political," he stated, "we can't do anything about it." "I don't want everything to be political." Seeing me burst into tears rendered him helpless. "Why cry?" he asked. How to know why? "We are comfortable," he continued. "We have everything to be happy for. Why are you crying?" "I have too many tears." "Too many tears? Come on!" "My novel is too sad." "They always finish happily, your novels." "That's what's so sad." "I don't understand you," he sighed. "Me neither."

"I would like to have been a Carmelite nun," I say. "You, a Carmelite nun? Hard to imagine..." "I would have sung hymns in a pure voice, carried candles, worn a cowl, with only my soul for beauty. I would have loved Jesus to madness. Or I'd have liked to be a courtesan." "Maria Magdalena, now." "Covered with men and jewels. Jesus loved her. She will be greatly forgiven because she loved a great deal." "His last temptation." "Lost in the world or outside it. A lost woman. Burned, burning, to the very end of my flame." "You're talking nonsense. Aren't you happy?" "And you?"

I lived in limbo, mechanically translating insipid novels. Nothing resembled life, yet it *was* life. Nothing resembled love in the least. Love, it seemed to me, should be a generous feeling. As so often happens, we failed to give enough. Yet sometimes there were tender words, considerate gestures, flowers on the table. Books lying about on the arms of chairs, music playing in the house.

Days go by, hair whitens, hands age, veins appear, sad wrinkles set in around the lips. The back begins to ache, teeth become loose. The voice acquires a hoarseness some find charming. The body becomes dry and brittle, like a bare tree in winter. One day the body no longer responds. I dread that day. Betrayal, sinking. Everything will have passed me by, I won't know how to have hung onto it. Balance: zero. I could have spent my life next to him without anything ever happening to us. I would have had an eventless life, a lifeless event. Sometimes sadness, sly and insidious, would creep into my chest, like a needle probing my ribs. I wasn't happy and yet I wasn't looking for happiness.

"How does the idea of aging strike you?"
"That's in the survey?" She is surprised.
"No."
"I'm scared of it, of course."
"And death?"
"I don't think about it."
"Why?"
"Because I don't want to die."
"I think about it all the time," I say.
"Why?"
"Because I don't want to die."
"We can't escape it."
"That's why I think about it."
"It doesn't help."
"I don't think of why, but of how. I worry about the way I'll die. I think of suffering."
"I'd like to go quickly," she declares. "I hope to feel nothing."
"I'm mostly scared of violence. I'm scared I'll be murdered."

"Oh. But why? Do you lead such a dangerous life?"
"All lives are dangerous. I'm scared of the violence of life."
"And you travel alone!"
"Violence is everywhere. Who can protect us?"
"Stop! I'll start to get scared too!"
"I want to die in a bed all in white, old and venerable, surrounded by love. I want my children and grandchildren to bend over to capture my last words."
"I don't want to die of AIDS," she says.
"Or burn to death."
"Or drown."
"Or die in an earthquake or an explosion. Or buried under rubble."
"Nor of hunger or thirst," she continues.
"Not in war. Not in a concentration camp."
"Not of cold."
"Not in a plane crash."
"Don't even mention it! You're asking for trouble."
"Not devoured by a lion, or squeezed to death and swallowed by a boa."
"How awful!"
"Not tortured, mutilated, my body hacked to pieces, buried in the woods, thrown in a green plastic bag at the end of a dead-end street."

These images would come to me when I watched the news on television. Philippe said: "You're obsessed with morbidity, poor darling." I protested: "What do you think? I do it on purpose? You heard the news, the same as I, you read the newspaper, right? You spend your life reading the newspaper. Does it leave *you* indifferent?" He exploded: "What's gotten into you? I'm not the one assassinating children!" He explained: "Whether I'm indifferent, as you say, or whether I cry doesn't change the facts." He went on: "It's as if you're making *me* responsible." And I answered yes, we are all responsible. But I didn't know in what way.

When he'd see me get depressed as I read about atrocities, he'd shake his head, dejected. He'd put his arm around my shoulders. To console me, he also told me it's always like that, as well you know, always the same thing, in every century, in every country of the world, no one is safe, it's always war in the twisted brains of some people. You just have to go on living. "As if nothing happened?" No, his words didn't console me. He continued: "You're too sensitive, poor darling. You have to take care of yourself." "To shield me, you mean?" "I mean don't let yourself get dragged down by morbidity." But I kept falling into it like mad, losing my footing, sliding downward. He turned off the television, took the paper out of my hands. "Come now, come to bed. You're falling over in exhaustion. Your nerves are shot." The next morning, bouquet in hand, and that apologetic smile. He felt he had caused me pain. More than anything he wanted to avoid making me suffer. My despair spilled onto him. He took me to a vegetarian restaurant. I put flowers on the table. We stopped talking about it.

In the days, I would spend long hours walking through the streets; I'd slink into the metro, emerge somewhere in the city and walk again, repeating to myself that no, I couldn't go on like this, translating sentimental novels, when life is so dark and children are being murdered, could not go on holding up a macho man ideal, smiling sardonically to readers while macho men beat and strangle their women, stab and shoot them, abandon their tortured bodies in the underbrush. It's there, in the newspaper every day an item appears that journalists call another family drama, the thirteenth of the year in the urban community. In describing macho men, I became an accomplice; this was how I became responsible. I passed in front of anonymous dwellings, tall apartment buildings that rose, all alike, along the sidewalks, and told myself it was perhaps behind one of those innocuous-looking facades that the horror was hidden. The city is full of those places that appear to be oases and are really pockets of despair.

"Why talk about it?" Claudine asks in an alarmed voice.

"You're right, why? Let's talk about love instead. Let's talk about Spain. About the sea."

"I've only been to the Atlantic," she says. "The eastern coast of the United States, the Maritimes. And the Caribbean."

"So turquoise, the Caribbean. The Mediterranean is mostly blue. It suggests something more... maternal. It always moves me. It's so old."

"I thought all seas were the same age."

"The age of the planet. But it's as if the Mediterranean has cradled humanity for a longer time than the others. Spain is old, too."

"Even the name makes me dream."

"The music, the matadors, the flamboyant colours. As a child I liked to imagine myself as Spanish."

"I was more ordinary. I dreamed I'd meet Prince Charming, that we'd get married and have a flock of children."

"And?"

"And no prince, I had to reconcile myself. But a part of my dream came true: I have a daughter."

I avert my eyes. They are filled with tears. Too much gin.

"She's twenty-one," she continues. "I would have liked her to come with me. But she couldn't miss three weeks of university classes... She's doing her Master's in psychology. Had we been able to predict Florent's accident, I would have settled for the week they pay for and taken her away with me."

"What's her name?"

"Julie. Do you have children?"

"A daughter too," I say.

"How old is she?"

"She isn't any age. She's dead. Had she lived, she'd be twenty-one, like yours. Perhaps they'd have gone to the same university, the same nightclubs."

Silence. This kind of revelation is always followed by silence. Silence, the only likely response. Someone tells you: "I lost my whole family in Auschwitz." You maintain a dismayed silence. You would rather have been deaf. You don't know where to look. Certainly not in this person's eyes, certainly not. More likely at the tips of your toes. A woman confides in a quavering voice: "My children all died in the same accident." A man tells you, his eyes filled with tears: "My wife has brain cancer. She's entered the terminal stage." All these are good reasons for remaining silent. But Claudine places her hand on my arm.

"Was it long ago?" she asks.

And I answer:

"Eighteen years."

"You never forget, do you?"

And I answer:

"Never."

Years pass and the scar is still raw. Never healed.

Her hand remains on my arm. She asks, but her voice is sad:

"How did it happen?"

And I answer:

"An accident."

Because the death of a child is always an accident. It cannot have been wanted, planned. Nothing can justify it, this gratuitous suffering. No explanation. No consolation.

She pours a bit more gin into our glasses.

"I don't think I could have survived," she says.

"I didn't really survive."

But that's not true. I did survive. I travelled, ate, read books, smoked cigarettes, loved men, walked through the streets, stayed in bars till closing, I swam in the sea, I screamed, I threw up after drinking too much, caught cold, laughed till I cried, petted cats. I put on makeup, I took bubble baths. I bought dresses and jewellery, I cooked, I made love. And I translated for the Love Collection. Survived.

The comedy is over. The screens go blank. In the plane, very little movement. A few lights remain on here and there: insomniacs reading or doing crossword puzzles. Claudine asks me if I'm tired. I'm not, but all this gin is making my head spin. I tell her I'm going to try to rest.

Complete silence. Just a lulling kind of humming, black night beyond the airplane window. That feeling that is always so reassuring of floating above the earth.

Small white pillow for my head. I huddle up, cramped, uncomfortable. What's the difference? To sleep for a few hours in this womb, like an anachronistic embryo. With the multitude of embryos, murmurs of sleep. Sleep.

Headphones on ears, inoffensive music with a civilizing influence. I close my eyes. My companion and I doze together, a blanket over our knees.

Chapter 2

> I am afraid of death, which is why I love life.
> Nijinsky, *Diary*

Here I am, naked and alone. Offering myself to the sea while she offers herself to me, face to face with her. Before life's blessing, this immovable untamed beauty of the sea, movement, power, constancy. And this has been given to me, like a charm, to rejoice in with all my senses. Here I am at the end of the earth, at the end of myself. I could just as well be before death.

As naked as the sea. And as alone. Despite a multitude of beings living and moving inside it. In myself as well, a multitude of beings and thoughts. Monsters inhabit its depths like they do mine; they roar, claw and destroy.

The sea fans out today, calm and turquoise. Beneath the sun, millions of sparks dance, a starry firmament. Only a diver could notice these monsters, were he to explore her depths. They have tentacles and warts, emerge from crevices, float around in the muck. Mine also move underground, but I feel them tremble when I dive inside myself.

I am naked because I've found a safe hiding place. I walk down the rocks, spread out a towel on the shingles, remove my clothes. Only a few birds see me and pay no attention. They fly, alighting for a moment on the crest of the waves, then open their wings and fly away again, never coming close to me. Their wings spread out, they fly above the waves, seeking prey. Their keen eyes detect a fish venturing too close to the surface. I hear their cries, my attention absorbed by experiences both minuscule and majestic, the surf, the intensity of the sun, the flight of seagulls, these signs of life.

Not really alone, though, because this presence fills me. What a racket, when the sea throws herself on the rocks, and at the same time, what silence! A tumultuous silence. It pervades until it sounds as if nothing else exists. *Does* anything else exist here? Singing, roaring, moaning, the call of the waves. Oh, to throw myself in and be swept away! The temptation of sinking into the sea.

In French, some people, strangely enough, refer to children as *"les flots,"* which means "waves." The first time I heard the expression, I was floored. "My *flot*, someone said. I have a *flot*." "Oh! Really? My, my. Personally I have a wave, a dune in my head." He'd laughed. "What are you talking about?" I'd answered: "And you?" I sought the meaning of the metaphor, believing it a very poetic way of expressing one's self. In truth, it *is* a very poetic way. A *flot*. Afterwards I thought it was perhaps a deformation of the word *fellow* and the charm dissolved.

I am naked before the sea, beneath the sun. You could not be more vulnerable. But I am fearless. If the sea carries me away, so be it; let her engulf me. The sea is like life, like death. When you look at her, you always want to be swept away in her sublime movement. You want to touch eternity. The body dragged down, sucked up, disappearing forever. You think it would be painless. But you have to hold back, deploy all your strength to resist its call. Only your mind breaks away and goes adrift. It glides – it too – like a bird. I breathe in deeply the sea air.

It was already day's end when I arrived here, three days ago, after two weeks of wandering. It's strange how

I felt no hurry to reach my destination. A kind of torpor enveloped me. I meandered from city to city, sleeping, according to my mood, in pensions or four star hotels. I swam in heated pools whose water was bitter with chlorinated staleness. In pensions, I rented a room furnished with a narrow, uncomfortable bed, a lopsided chest of drawers, a sink with only one tap, cold water of course, a plywood closet containing three misshapen hangers. Often my window would look out over a patio decorated with bougainvillea and potted geraniums. In the morning I'd notice birds pecking at the thick grass, quenching their thirst in the birdbath.

In the hotels I had an armchair, a table, a telephone near the bed; I would have my own bathroom, with small cakes of soap in their soft pink wrapping, a downy pile of towels, plenty of hot water. I revelled in it, I spent hours in the bathtub. I would lie down on the big bed and turn on the television to put me to sleep. The images flowed by, the music of foreign voices soothed me. I would sleep an hour, wake up, go back to sleep.

I would eat in my room: bread and cheese, green apples. I drank water and wine. I could just as well have let myself die from starvation. It was an imitation of life, a line barely moving across a hospital screen in the intensive care unit. I was without hope. What effort it took to get out of bed, leave the room and emerge resplendent in the sun! I always wore dark glasses.

I would take one street, then another, going into a bakery, a tobacconist, examining the postcards on their metal racks, buying cigarettes. I smoked in the street. I walked in parks. I would sit down on a bench, immobile for hours, watching the crowd pass, a continuous wave. Who were all these people? What stories did they carry within, what tragedies lay in their hearts? Inventing people's lives was my afternoon activity. This passer-by would become a runaway terrorist, this woman, looking as if she'd been plunged into mourning, must have lost her entire family in the fire that ravaged her home; another suffered from a cruel, incurable disease. Sometimes, but more rarely, I would imagine happy lives. Swarms of laughing teenagers passing by, school bags under their arms, children bursting out laughing on the swings, a little old lady dressed all in black feeding the pigeons who recognized her: serene signs of everyday life. I would choose a character among these and offer him a gift, a holiday existence: a hand caressing his hair, the purring of a cat, a piano in a room bathed in light. Notes chiming from the window: the little old lady had been an acclaimed musician, I could hear bursts of wild applause from everywhere, she arose and bowed to the audience, her dress white and sparkling, her shoulders bare, her severe bun transformed into luxuriant hair held in place by a mother-of-pearl barrette in back. A lover, a husband overcome with emotion waited in the wings. She ran to seek refuge in his arms. The wool of his jacket, this slightly harsh warmth against her cheek, comforted her. Simple gifts life can offer in its bounty – I gave them to the bird woman, then returned, a little lighter, to the hotel. I made resolutions: to go out, sit outdoors at a restaurant and order a good meal, go to the movies, go dancing, let myself be wooed by a handsome, dark man, bring him back to my hotel. In his arms, love, like fireworks. But I always ended up going to bed without going out. After two weeks of wandering, I went into a bus station and chose Almuñecar among the destinations written on the large board. I remembered having already passed by this city, a coastal resort quasi-deserted at this time of year. I left the same afternoon.

    Coming out of the bus station, I got my bearings. I looked for the sea. There would surely be apartments to rent on the Paseo. At this late hour, I should hurry to find a roof over my head. I didn't want to take a taxi, but to discover the place on my own, get a feel for it. I didn't make any inquiries. I walked with assurance, as if I lived there.

I walked along the seashore. The sun was on the point of setting and the light had a special quality, the softness it has at dusk when it has been nice all day. Warm and dewy, not intense, but muted, everything delicate. A watermarked crescent of a moon, an ironic smile in the pale sky.

I liked the sounds and smells, the apparent serenity of the place. I would be at home here, nesting, like on an island.

The building was called "Ultima Ola," as if the last wave had just come there to die. I chose it for its name. A garden surrounded it, an orange cat perched nonchalantly on the edge of the empty pool. A sign at the entrance advertised apartments for rent.

The rental office was still open. I entered. Inside, seated behind a cluttered desk, a faraway look in his eyes, a tall, thin young man with dark curly hair, wearing a blue checked shirt, was daydreaming. I explained in a few words what I was looking for, and he showed me an apartment overlooking the sea, on the third floor. We came back downstairs. I filled out forms, showed my passport, paid the first month's rent. He handed over the keys. I asked him his name. Manuel. But people call him Manolo.

Then I took possession of the place: made the bed, lay down between the sheets, placed my toothbrush and cleansing cream on the shelf above the bathroom sink, drank a glass of water in the kitchen, smoked a cigarette. Now the place is lived in. Because although I want to remain anonymous, the places I choose to live in still have to resemble me, I want to recognize my scent, my gestures, see cigarette butts in the ashtray, my cleanser in the bathroom, a hair of mine on the pillow. I am an animal marking its territory.

Then I went to the grocery, nearby. I bought bread, wine, tomatoes, oranges, olives. Five different kinds. I stayed a few minutes sitting on the little wall bordering the beach in front of the building, eating black and green olives, the ones stuffed with almonds, the pitted *manzanillas*, the ones marinated in garlic and lemon. I heard the sea at my back, I watched the people out for an evening walk. I repeated to myself: I have the sea at my back, I am eating Spanish olives in Spain, in front of where I live. Can this resemble happiness? A certain kind of contentment, at least? I came to this destination, I told myself. I am on solid ground, have a fixed address, an official dwelling. Edificio Ultima Ola, apartamento 303, Paseo Reina Sofia. I am home. I can begin work.

Once inside, I opened the cupboards, counted the glasses and plates, inspected the contents of the drawers: four knives, six spoons, four forks, a corkscrew, a can opener, a whisk, a spatula. I could even make friends and invite them to dinner. I would impress them with recipes from the magazine, the smoked salmon omelette, exotic salad, mandarin mousse. I also found a set of stained pans, two beat-up pots, a blue earthenware pitcher, an espresso maker, and no cockroaches.

White sheets were in the chest of drawers, a woollen blanket in the closet, towels neatly folded on top of the toilet in the bathroom, watercolour seascapes hanging on the living room wall, as if the view of the sea alone were not enough. I sliced tomatoes and bread, uncorked a bottle of wine, and sat down at the table on the balcony.

Later, night fell, definitively, covering the sea and trees. Water crashed over the rocks. I willed away anxiety, rejected it. The crashing of the water drowned out all possible voices. The bottle of wine was empty and I didn't notice time pass. I locked the front door, but opened wide the one leading to the balcony. In the distance, a point jutted out into the sea. A lighthouse rose from it, flashing at steady intervals in the night. When I lay down on the couch, I couldn't see the street, only the beam of the lighthouse, the waves and the tops of the palm trees. The moon, on the water, traced a trail of light. It feels as if I'm living in a boat that the wind is pushing toward an island. I abandon myself, languorously. Sometimes drifting is salutary.

The next day I walked to the heart of the village, bought Spanish newspapers, T-shirts of every colour featuring Almuñecar, the rocks, the castle, the sailboats on the water, the fishing boats on shore, I bought jeans, a warm sweater, and an inexpensive cassette tape. In a secondhand bookstore, I found a battered French-English dictionary. I also bought good lined notebooks made of entirely recycled paper, their pretty covers decorated with musical staffs, extra-fine-tipped blue pens. Coming home, I moved some of the furniture around, took down the watercolours and stored them in the cupboard. The seascape is live before my eyes.

And now I am here, completely naked, hidden by the rocks. Completely naked and alone.

Sometimes very powerful odours emanate from the sea. Dead fish, decomposing algae, shells. Forceful odours. They seem to come from the very belly of the sea. They trouble and keel the brain. That's how Leonard Ming spoke. Leonard Ming, the Man from Hong Kong, the killer. The ocean that soothes me fed his furor. The odour of death reminded him of that which stagnates around ports in the morning, when the fishing boats come in.

He is dead now. The killer is no more, killed in turn, but in the electric chair, following an interminable, widely publicized trial. His autobiography was a sensation. He wrote in his cell, condemned to die, leaving out no detail. I came away on this trip to translate this man's story. I gave up on the Love Collection, the lies of romance.

I decided to enter death and its truth. I wanted to do it all alone, near the sea and consoled by her. Naked on the rocks, I breathe in the salty air to infinity, as if iodine could heal the heart.

Chapter 3

> I know everything, without having been at the scene of the crime.
>
> Nijinsky, *Diary*

Right now my head is spinning. Two sleepless nights, interspersed with afternoons on the rocks. On the table, the remains of a meal: crumbs, pits, peelings, a glass of water. Also on the table, the book with the glossy black cover. Its bloody lettering assaults the eyes. Its title, *Wolfman*, in blood red. The author, Leonard Ming, the decade's most notorious killer.

I, who by and large feel affection for both men and wolves, intend to suggest *Thanatos* as the title for the French version. But I know the publishers will find my title too interpretive, intellectual, not saleable. I know they'll prefer *L'Homme-loup*, a literal translation.

I've read it through. I spent two nights straining my eyes, underlining difficult words, obscure passages. In a frame of mind close to detachment. Exhaustion and detachment. In this case, it's a cause and effect relationship. Sometimes exhaustion leads to vulnerability, hyper emotionalism. Nothing like that now. I'm a little dizzy, but with fatigue. I haven't entered death, not yet. I stayed at the surface of the words, translating from one language to the other. I haven't yet penetrated their meaning.

Now I know everything, I know the facts. Birth of Leonard Ming in Hong Kong into a wealthy family. Father a Chinese businessman, British mother. Five children – he was the third. Elementary school in Hong Kong, secondary school in Yorkshire. Return to Hong Kong at the age of sixteen. Facts, dates. The itinerary of a human being. He in fact speaks very little of his childhood, except to say that very young he developed a taste for cruelty. He always had a taste for blood; even as a child he tortured cats and birds. Flesh-eater, carnivore, cannibal: he was all that. Erect in the middle of a mass grave, dressed in black, triumphant, that was how he saw himself. Holding a bird in his hand and slowly poking out its eyes with a needle, feeling the bird flutter wildly, he knew sensuality. He enjoyed loitering outside slaughterhouses. There was a smell there that drove him wild. A racket too: howling, bellowing, protesting, crying. All senses awakened. Pleasures of the senses. He was very young; this was the sensuality of his childhood. Afterwards, he sought out these sensations and looked for variations. "No kill, no thrill" was one of his favourite expressions. He had written these words in jest, with a trace of humour. I underlined the expression. I would have to find an equivalent in French. "*Quand on ne tue pas, on ne jouit pas,*" perhaps. "When you don't kill, you don't come," maybe? No, too long. And in English the sounds crack like a whip. "*Tuer, c'est le pied*"? "Killing for Kicks"? I don't like that either. But do I like "No kill, no thrill"? Other similar expressions crop up in the text. "No gun, no fun." "Mommy cries, Daddy dies, Baby cries." I underlined them as well. I'll come up with a translation later. For now, the sun has been up a long time, my eyes are burning, but I'm not sleepy.

I closed the book. I am empty. Impervious to emotion. Too tired. I'm going to leave my lair, walk along the Paseo, brush past those walking by, the women on their way to market, the morning joggers.

But before, when I take my shower, I'll let the hot water run over me for a long time.

I put on my long écru cotton dress. I must be the only woman in this city dressed like this. The others wear pale blouses, straight dresses above the knee. Or jeans and sweaters. I found this dress in Montreal in a used clothing store, and seeing it awoke in me a desire to travel. Suspended from a hanger in the dead of winter, it seemed to yearn for faraway lands.

In a large bag I put a beach towel and yesterday's newspaper which I won't read.

My path is lined with shut down hotels, practically empty buildings, quasi-deserted restaurants. Off-season. A little farther on beats the heart of the city: banks, a post office, all kinds of stores, a school filled with the screeching of children, the market. Before reaching it, I spot palmettos, cleverly aligned at the foot of the rocky wall; I pass gardeners, line fishermen, men with hearty complexions repairing fishing nets, repainting small crafts red or orange. Here and there birds in their cages sing at the top of their lungs; perhaps they are calling for help. That's what I would do if I were a bird shut up in a cage. Or else I'd bury my head under my wings, a small ball of feathers curled up, and no one would hear from me again. Suddenly an image crops up, violent and raw: Leonard Ming, as a child in Hong Kong, jabbing a needle into the eyes of a bird.

On the flower-laden balconies I see the bare shoulders of women sunbathing.

Old people pass, taking small steps, walking their dogs. All kinds of dogs. Elegant hounds, Great Danes with their almost-frightening bodies, obscene, crazy poodles, their eyes like shiny marbles, black beneath their tousled hair, despondent-looking spaniels, but mostly stubby, plump mongrels on four legs, shorthaired, black and white. Well-behaved for the most part, they never bark or pull on their leashes. Stray dogs sometimes latch onto passers-by. Scrawny cats loiter around the few clients seated on restaurant terraces. People throw mouthfuls of fish, bread, gristle from chicken. Cats sidle up to them, ears down, devouring the mouthful as if fearing it would be snatched from them, as if it were the first or last of their lives. I smile at the sight. I like all cats, even the mangy-looking ones who beg on the restaurant terraces. Their role of beggar does not diminish their arrogance.

Parked trailers gleam, their bodywork shining, curtains closed. Their licence plates are Belgian, German. Pregnant women wear dark glasses, others push children in strollers or invalids in wheelchairs. Settled in front of the sea, the disabled meditate. A simpleton throws food wrappings in the waves and laughs alone, a crazy woman stamps her foot and wails, but no one pays any attention.

I settle down at a restaurant terrace on the beach. I order *café con leche*. I light a cigarette, open my journal at random. I have my dark glasses, nobody can see I'm not reading. My eyes are tired.

Suddenly I hear: "May I keep you company?" A voice is speaking to me, the hint of a lilting accent.

A man is standing in front of me, a man smiling broadly, one hand resting on the back of the white chair across from me. He is tall, with dark hair, tanned. My type, in fact, tall, dark, tanned. Mediterranean. I wonder why he is speaking to me in French. He is waiting for me to accept his company.

"Sit down, if you like," I say without smiling.

"We were on the same plane" he informs me.

The waiter approaches and the man orders black coffee.

"My name is Lukas," he continues. "It's not an Italian name, but I was born in Naples."

He emigrated to Canada at the age of three. We were travelling on the same plane because he had been visiting his parents in Toronto. He lives in Rome.

I listen to this without too much surprise.

"Don't you want to know what I'm doing here?"

"I'm not curious, but if you insist, I'll certainly ask you."

"You're not helping me very much."

"No."

"Would you like another cup of coffee?" he suggests. "Would you like something else? A drink, perhaps?"

"A curaçao."

He motions to the waiter.

"And now," he says, "may I ask *you*?"

"What?"

"What brings you to Almuñecar?"

"It's a pretty city."

They bring the curaçao.

"You don't look as if you're... on vacation."

"I'm not. And you?"

"Finally you're showing a bit of interest in me. To tell you the truth, I'm not on vacation either. I've had a house built here, in Cotobro. I've come to keep an eye on things during the final stages."

"Cotobro?"

"Up on the hill."

"There's a song like that."

"Yes?"

I hum: "Up on the hill, people never stare..."

"You're funny."

"Not always. Rarely, in fact."

"I was sitting right in front of you in the airplane. I heard a bit of your conversation."

"Was it funny?"

"Not always. But I didn't hear everything."

"No?"

"I didn't want to pry. I didn't know you. I found your conversation more interesting than the film."

"You heard that I'd come to translate a book?"
"Yes."
"Yet you just asked me what I'm doing here."
"To break the ice. I was surprised to see you again. It was completely unexpected."
"Does that change anything?"
"I'm delighted. At the same time, seeing you again intimidates me. You are, in a way, not exactly a stranger. To be frank, I was hoping to see you again."
"You were hoping to?"
"Hoping without hope. A little daydream rather than an obsession. I like to hear women speak," he continued. "Hear them without their knowing. I am something of a voyeur, but I use my ears. An eavesdropper, if you will. At one point you used an expression that intrigued me, that I liked. You said there are other fish in the sea. I liked that, a kind of offhand way of presenting things. It was direct and nice."
"I am not a nice woman. Nor offhand. The opposite is true."
"I think that you are. Nice, I mean. Offhand, too, in a way. I thought of you often."
"Thought of me?"
"You kept returning to my thoughts. I was sitting in front of you in the plane. I heard your voice, but couldn't see you. My curiosity was aroused and I went to get something to drink so I could see your face on the way back. You were next to the window and it was dark, but I got an idea. Afterwards, listening to you took on another dimension. At one point, you went to get soda and ice cubes with your friend. I got up and was able to see your body. Quickly, fleetingly. But I saw how you walked, how you moved in the confined space of the aisle."
"Why are you telling me this?"
"To explain that I was thinking of you. I was hoping you'd say where you were going in Spain, but you didn't

know. You spoke of Andalusia. It was vague, but gave me a little hope. I knew you wouldn't go to Marbella. That relieved me – that place revolts me. I understood that you were here to translate a book, a romance novel."

"Yes."

I don't disillusion him. I don't tell him about the autobiography of the killer. I act as if I spend my life in sugar-coated stories.

"Would you like another curaçao?" he inquires. "Would you like to eat something? To go for a walk? I have my car. Do you know the area?"

"Not really."

"There is a small town about twenty kilometres from here called Maro. We could go there. The beach is very pretty."

"I have work," I say.

"Of course."

"But I'll do it tonight. I always work at night."

In Maro, standing up at the counter of a deserted bar, we have another cup of coffee, then take the steep, dusty trail leading to the beach. We remove our shoes and walk along the rough, greyish sand strewn with pebbles and rusty beer and Coca-Cola cans.

I watch him as he walks alongside me. I let my mind drift. I think his body must be warm, smooth, comfortable, that his voice is reassuring as well as his silence. A man's voice, a man's body. Full of life, like a tree. Hard as a tree, and fragrant. Well-rooted, planted firmly on the ground. Heavy, I imagine the weight of his body on mine, heavy and light at the same time. Sweaty during love, emitting a slightly salty smell. I imagine his firm thighs locking mine, feel their hardness. The sight of his broad shoulders beneath his shirt excites me. We stop walking for a moment. I look into his eyes and imagine his sex. The thought comes to me and lingers a while.

I do not speak to him about a killer and his victims: babies, little children, teenagers, women, men shut up in a bunker somewhere in a northern California settlement, I don't ask him what he thinks of it, but I think about it endlessly. I'm afraid to mention this to him, that he'll answer me the way Philippe did, telling me I'm obsessed with morbidity.

For two nights I read, thinking myself detached, but now the images rain down upon me and I shiver and suddenly various parts of my body ache. In my left breast most of all, because of the passage in which Leonard Ming describes how, with a carving knife, he cut off the left nipple of a girl. Faces contorted, howling, begging, distorted by pain, spin round me while the body of this man standing before me makes me shudder. Confused impressions, cold sweat, then heat. Contradictory sensations. What is making me dizzy? The body of a man standing before me is making me dizzy. Somewhere else in the world, a woman's nipple is being sliced off. But that's what's making me dizzy: the simultaneity of pleasure and pain.

"You don't look well," he says.

"Probably because I'm tired. I haven't slept yet. And I drank too much coffee."

"Would you prefer to go back and rest?"

"Yes."

We take the path in the opposite direction, bare feet in the wet sand, and as we walk, our footsteps, like those of separated lovers, are obliterated by the sea. We climb back up the steep, dusty trail and he slides a hand under my arm. I remain silent. Ever since I read Leonard Ming, since I agreed to translate his story, I feel an excess of guilt, have the impression I'm carrying a secret I can't reveal. I have the impression that if I speak, I'll betray myself, a certain look, a quavering voice, will betray me. He'll realize I know something he doesn't.

Afterwards, he drops me off in front of the Ultima Ola. He suggests coming back to fetch me later, that evening. We could eat together in a restaurant on the beach.

"I don't know," I say. "I don't really feel like going out in the evening. I work all night. I'm very tired. And above all I need solitude."

He insists: he has to go back to Rome soon. He insists that we still have things to tell each other.

We make a date for nine o'clock. I walk upstairs to my place. I look at my work table, the book I have to start translating, the notebook with its cover decorated with musical staffs, the blue pen. I put two oranges in my bag, then go out to walk on the beach. I find my hiding place among the rocks, sit down in front of the sea. And now, suddenly and for no reason, I am invaded by a violent sensation of loss. Is it really for no reason? Aren't I, on the contrary, completely lost, abandoned? And even if it is I who wanted it this way, does it change anything? I am cold. The crashing of the waves becomes unbearable. It never stops, ever. I want the waves to be still for a moment. They no longer reassure me, no longer comfort me. I only want to hear silence, genuine silence. I tremble. I am so cold. I close my eyes. Lukas's face appears behind my eyelids. A buoy, I hang on. A man's body. I must give face to desire, so that my desire rescues me. I need something concrete. Need to name what could fill the void. Lukas. When I say the name in my head, I name desire. I want the face, the body of a man to fill the space between the chasm and myself, want them to intercept and break my fall. I must erase the faces of Leonard Ming and his victims, the images of the bunker, of bones unearthed in the ground surrounding the house, instruments and weapons – the book contains eight full pages of raw photos, hideous, in black and white on glossy paper.

The body is everything, everything is physical. Pain and joy are in the body. A man and a woman can act with gentleness, they can be lovers. A man may be a gardener, his hands caring for plants and flowers. His hands may caress the skin of a woman, milk a goat, run across the keyboard of a piano, his fingers lovingly pinch the strings of a guitar, holding it to his heart and leaning over it. His hands can gag, brandish a weapon, his nails scratch, his teeth bite till the blood comes out. He becomes a killer. Is he the same man? With his voice, he can speak of simple things, hum a tune heard on the radio, with his voice he can utter the most humiliating insults, he can taunt. Is it the same voice? How vulnerable the body, how it desires and fears. In the world, people enjoy and suffer simultaneously. Pain and pleasure trace parallel paths. The earth, like one singular body simultaneously experiencing ecstasy and agony.

I calm down. I invent gestures, always the same, a knee sliding between mine and opening them, a hand resting on the nape of my neck; inventing this reassures me. An endless array of tender gestures and acceptance. Opening the body, the heart, opening everything, letting in life. A face leans over me and it is Lukas. These gestures alone can prevent my fall through the chasm. The pressure of a knee between mine, I open myself, accepting, desiring, gripping his shoulders to receive the love of a man the way you receive life.

I rest my head against the rock. These gestures alone can make me forget. The faces of the victims finally blur, fade away; for a moment, a man's body takes their place. The whining dies down, replaced by a man's words of love. The pain in my left breast eases up. A man's hand caresses it gently. A man's mouth settles on the nipple. A man's lips suck on it, a man's tongue glides over it, a man's saliva moistens it. I am a Love Collection reader, I tell myself: just for a moment, to be this reader and abandon myself to this dream, this pleasure. I desire this strong man, want to quiver in his arms. His thigh, I want to feel it against me, his sex hard against my stomach.

His heart, I want to feel it beat against my chest, I want to annihilate death in the arms of this man.

Fleeting, this moment of desire before the sea. Because nothing ever erases anything.

I don't have to live through the experience. It all happens in my head; it all will stay in my head and no one will know anything about it.

I get up, leave my hiding place, walk along the Paseo. At intervals, the beach is lower, I don't know why, stone steps lead down to the sea. Sometimes, like today, I settle down there with a newspaper, or scribble in a notebook letters I don't send.

My mind absent, gliding over the waves.

I sit on the steps. I stay there.

Suddenly I feel something brush against my arm. A man is sitting next to me. I didn't hear him arrive. In his sixties, gold-rimmed glasses, head of thinning grey hair. Elegant in his bucks, impeccably creased striped wool pants, carefully ironed white shirt, understated tie and suede jacket. He greets me. He introduces himself: Abelardo. He asks me my name. I tell him in Spanish. From his balcony, he tells me, while he was looking out at the horizon with his binoculars, he took me for a Madonna of the sea.

"A Madonna?"

I burst out laughing.

"Yes, a mermaid, a mirage. Because of the dress."

I show him my feet.

"You see I lack something a mermaid needs."

"It's good to hear laughter," he sighs.

He continues: he came down from Madrid to spend a few days in peace. Am I married? he inquires. No, unmarried. He, yes. The shadow of a bitter smile. Life with his wife, he explains, has become a constant war, screaming and confrontations. He has had it. He tells me his life, laid bare, just like that, with no introduction. He buries his head in his hands. Can I imagine, he asks, forty years of life together, having four children, four grandchildren, and ending up like that?

A faint scent of cologne hovers in the air.

Then he asks me to excuse him. He needed to talk. Perhaps he is disturbing me. In Spanish, they say *molestar*. I shiver hearing this word. I answer no, he isn't disturbing me, molesting me. He noticed me from his balcony and couldn't resist the temptation of coming down. Here, like in Madrid, he has no one in whom to confide. No one but old pensioners, both men and women, come here to finish their insignificant lives. When they are foreigners, they don't even take the trouble to learn Spanish. "In winter this town is a deathtrap, you know," he concludes.

I know.

The people come here for the mild climate. They are old, come here with their old age and their dogs, then die and their dogs stray, distraught, on the Paseo and on the beach. And when the dogs die first, their owners are inconsolable. It's unbelievable, the number of people who die here, haven't I heard tell of it? I answer no, not specifically, but that people die everywhere, both peacefully and violently. Might as well choose to go peacefully.

In his building, he continues, lived an old Dutch woman, at least ninety years old. She fed all the stray cats in the area. She had collected a half dozen that she kept in her home. For years, she worked as a volunteer for the veterinarian. He learned of her death when he got here. That's how it is, people come here to die. Like waves, they die in the sun, snuffed out peacefully, like candles whose wicks have been used up. I question him: what will happen to the cats? He shrugs his shoulders, showing his powerlessness. Or indifference. The cats were put back in the street. They in turn will become stray cats and others will feed them.

And me, he asks, at my age, I'm certainly not retired, what am I doing here?

"More or less the same thing," I tell him.
He doesn't seem to understand.
"What do you do?"
"I do nothing."
"Oh! On vacation?"
"In a way."
"And you chose Almuñecar?"
"For its mild climate."

After a brief silence, he repeats that no, it can't go on anymore, he must change his life, must live before it's too late. He buries his head in his hands and sighs: "*¡Dios mio! ¡Dios mio!*"

I no longer know if he's addressing me or himself. Or else this God, who ignores him. He says he wants to travel, to visit all the chateaux, the cathedrals of Spain, that he'd like to take a play subscription for a season, a concert subscription, do simple, pleasant things, but with a companion. He needs a woman. With his wife, everything has become impossible, everything always ends in scenes of recrimination.

He says that when he bought the condominium he didn't know that Almuñecar was a deathtrap. Now he's thinking of selling it. He didn't know that there were only old people in the building, only old people with their canes, their wheelchairs, their sicknesses, it's like a hospital, an old-age home. So you see, by a sort of osmosis, he feels old himself.

He isn't very young, evidently, but I avoid rubbing salt in the wound.

I don't even understand why he's telling me all this, why he's flaunting his bitterness in my face. I simply wanted to be here, with my anonymous desire, in front of the sea. This man's presence makes the desire recede. Sourness, sadness, and dreariness intervene, tarnishing it. The brilliance has disappeared.

He informs me that he was a banker, for a long time the manager of a large branch of the *Banco Popular* in

Madrid. He retired last year. Now he realizes that he worked too much, from a very young age, without any respite. He didn't notice time pass and now, it has passed. He wants to enjoy life, the years that remain, can I understand that?

I can understand, even though I don't know what kind of enjoyment he's talking about. I can still understand that people desire love, dream of castles and experiencing vistas and music with a loved one.

The wind blowing in off the ocean is becoming increasingly cold. I decide to go home. Abelardo walks me to my door.

Once back home, I think about these words, that people come here to die. The wind blows violently. From the balcony door, I observe the tops of the palm trees, looking like hair being yanked. The sea is so full she looks as if she is trying to burst into the house. The waves hurl themselves beyond the little wall, splashing onto the Paseo. A flock of noisy gulls hovers close to the waves.

Nothing, though, evokes death here. I think of the little old ladies feeding the cats, now ensconced in their homes, watching the sea swell like a threat, the palm trees shake, and I tell myself that I am just like them, loving cats and ensconced in my home.

And I too have come here for a meeting with death.

I heat some milk, melt a sugar cube. *Comfort food*, they call it in English. Food that comforts and consoles. Warm milk and cookies, like when as a child you were sick, when you had a nightmare and cried out in the night. Warm milk with cookies and honey, sometimes, before going to bed. In pale pink flannel pyjamas patterned with teddy bears and rabbits, your feet in furry slippers. Warm milk in winter, before going to sleep, while your mother, alongside you, tells a story from the picture book illustrated with silky-haired princesses, courageous princes, enchanted bluebirds, talking frogs. "Sleep well, sweet dreams." The picture book is closed, put back on the shelves above the bureau, the empty cup removed, the bedside light turned off, but the lovestruck princes, the bighearted pirates, the brave princesses continue to move about in the shadows. They are getting ready for the ball while generous fairies lean over cradles, arms laden with gifts. I will give you beauty, I will give you kindness, I will give you love.

Stretched out on the couch, two cushions beneath my head, I set my cup on the cold flagstone floor. I think of the cold dark bunker that Leonard Ming and his accomplice Gary Sheldon built next to the house in Wilseyville, near San Andreas, California. I will, of course, keep the word *bunker* in the French version. But I could translate it to mean cage, hiding place, jail, hole, dungeon.

The bunker was divided into two rooms; the first, quite roomy and comfortably furnished, conceived of as a shelter, since Sheldon had a phobia of imminent nuclear war. In the book, a photo shows a double bed, a heating plate holding a pan, two pots; a small refrigerator, a counter above which are cupboards whose open doors reveal tinned food, peas, beef stew, condensed milk, bags of rice and pasta, liquor bottles, jars of instant coffee. Shelves with a few books whose titles can't be made out, a television set. The other room was a camouflaged cell, sparsely furnished, a straw mattress without sheets on the concrete floor, upside-down crates. A two-way mirror allowed the tormentors to observe their despairing, terrified prisoners. The photo also shows chains and iron rings affixed to the wall.

Following the ritual of hot milk, when I was a child, princes clad in purple velvet bowed in my bedroom before damsels whose silky hair fell to their knees; goodhearted pirates rescued noble ladies from the violent waves, intrepid knights fought dragons. There would be a shepherd daydreaming in a sun-drenched field, a lamb in his arms. Golden rings were magic, swords were enchanted, good genies appeared out of lamps to grant wishes. And evil was always defeated.

Now, after the hot milk, it is bound men who grimace, mutilated women who bleed and beg, terrified children who stare at me.

But no one comes to rescue them.

Chapter 4

> I do not seek novels when I read novels, but truth.
> Nijinsky, *Diary*

The bell pulls me from sleep. I get up, glance at the balcony door. The wind has died down and the full moon casts a billowing, silvery sheet over the sea.

I open the door. Lukas is there, smiling. It seems as if this man is always smiling.

"I'm not ready," I say. "I fell asleep."

"Take your time."

He comes in. Near the door, we kiss on the cheek, the way all civilized people do.

"You've kept on your dress. It suits you. I forgot to tell you that before."

He follows me into the living room. I offer him Malaga wine. I put on a Dead Can Dance cassette.

"It's very feminine," he says.

"The music?"

"The dress."

"I'm going to disappoint you. This dress is for daytime. In the evening I always wear jeans and a sweater."

"At this time of year, here in Spain, the evenings are too cool for dresses."

I leave him to go get changed. In the bathroom, I brush my teeth and hair. I put rouge on my lips, mascara on my eyelashes. When I come back into the living room, Lukas has the book in his hands.

"Is this what you call 'the Love Collection'?"

"No."
I finish my glass of wine standing up, then turn my back to get my purse and the worn leather jacket that I bought at the market. I remain standing near the living room door until he puts the book back on the table and gets up. We leave the apartment.

"You didn't turn off the cassette," he says.

"I don't want to interrupt the music. That kind of behaviour is an affront to the musicians. I like the idea that the music goes on after I leave, that it lives on at home while I'm gone. When it's not a tape, but the radio that is on, I feel as if I'm being greeted when I come back in. Sometimes I hear flamenco, or Chopin, as if a musician awaited me in the living room."

We get into the car. He turns on the radio.

"Here is some music to welcome you on board..."

"Here is my refuge," I say as we pass in front of my hiding place.

"Your refuge?"

"I come here every afternoon. Below, hidden by the rocks, I found a little creek, an isolated beach."

"Have no fear, I won't come here to disturb you... When I used to come to Almuñecar," he continues, "these buildings weren't here. Nor was the Paseo. They dynamited the mountain and stole this space from the sea."

"They're still dynamiting the mountain."

"Now they're building a breakwater."

"Still trying to contain the sea's appetite?"

"When the wind blows from the east, there is practically no beach in front of your building. Sometimes the water rises above the wall... Thirty years ago, Almuñecar was just a small farming and fishing village. Also a vacation spot, but not well-known. There was rain then, and the countryside was green. Women washed clothes in the Rio Verde."

"Now the river is completely dry."

"It doesn't rain anymore. The region is becoming a desert. There are all kinds of theories to explain the phenomenon."

"Yes, I know, a butterfly beating its wings in China."

"That one, and others. A volcanic eruption in Japan, a fire that devastated the forest here at the beginning of the seventies…"

"You've been coming to Almuñecar for thirty years?"

"My parents missed Europe. For them, travelling was a priority. They saved all year, and in summer, we would leave on vacation. Once it was Spain. I wasn't impressed at first, but over time, the memory of Almuñecar took hold and I began to dream of owning a house here. When the city began to develop, I was still a very naive young man. I was taken in by a swindler. He sold the same land to several suckers like myself. He was a Canadian. I trusted him, a compatriot, you can imagine. Believe it or not, his wife's name was Marie-Crucifix. How could I have been suspicious? He lived like a king here in Almuñecar, gave parties to which the mayor, the local priest, and owners of small businesses were invited. Everyone respected him. Even today, people still speak of Edmond Lacerte with a certain amused admiration."

"Edmond Lacerte…"

"He brought work, a sort of vision of modernity and prosperity. He ended his days in prison."

"Here in Spain?"

"Yes, here, in Granada… He had four or five children. One of his daughters stayed on. She married a gypsy. In the mornings she sells grilled sardines at the marketplace."

"Oh! But I've seen that woman. A redhead with long hair?"

"That's her. Barbara."

"Funny kind of destiny for the daughter of a man who once was king."

A Sevillian song is playing on the radio. I burst out laughing.

"What's so funny?"

"The Canadian swindler. I find the idea completely outrageous. You don't imagine Canadians as international swindlers, as spies, terrorists, guerrilla fighters."

"It's true that the image we project is usually more placid."

"You imagine them as senior citizens playing tourist, a little clumsy, coming out of air-conditioned buses, wearing white hats with fluorescent visors. Or else as young backpackers, broke, slumping on squares in front of cathedrals, strumming their guitars and humming Simon and Garfunkel and Leonard Cohen in slow, gentle voices. Looking as though they're never sure of themselves, smiling kindly and always forcing themselves to stumble through a few words of the language of whatever country they're in. 'Nice people,' as they say."

"That's not a crime."

"Oh no! They are conciliatory, full of goodwill when they go abroad."

"That's how *you* imagine them. I know some who constantly criticize."

"Maybe, but I'm speaking of general perception. Hospitable when they entertain guests at home, always ready to get out the good tablecloth, to let people sample the native products, maple syrup, blueberry pie, the deep-dish meat pie from Lac Saint-Jean called *tourtière*, offering their forests, lakes, and rivers to foreign hunters and fishermen, their bears, their moose, their caribou, their salmon and their trout. Contorting their mouths to speak properly so that foreigners will understand them. Grateful when foreigners come to pillage their oceans, their lakes, their rivers, their forests. Thanks for appreciating our products, want some more?"

"You *are* cynical. Perhaps that was true at one time, but things have changed. It's not like that anymore."

"You think so? Aren't they always ready to roll out the red carpet for foreign singers, for writers, dancers, painters, conference speakers, all kinds of prominent foreigners, marvelling naively that these singers, dancers, painters, conference speakers, all these prominent people have condescended to visit their uncivilized country? And always vaguely guilty: for having mistreated Aboriginal Peoples, for slaughtering baby seals, for lacking culture, for not using the right words, for having a provincial-sounding accent, for not having known how to attract enough immigrants, enough investors, for not having enough famous actors or Nobel Prize winners, for not having had a glorious past, with heroes admired throughout the world, except for little Anne in her green-gabled house. Not like the Americans who arrive like conquerors…"

"We're also from America."

"I mean the ones from the States… And not like the Germans, the French, or the British. No, rather timid at the money exchange with their dollar that is worth so much less than the other. Always polite, capable of saying 'excuse me' in every language."

"You're exaggerating. I don't feel that way at all."

"You aren't Canadian."

"I have Canadian citizenship."

"Are you proud of it?"

"I'd say so."

"Of course you were raised in Toronto, that explains everything. And Canada, for your parents, was the New World. In Quebec, we are more disillusioned… To continue with my perception of Canadians…"

"Yes?"

"Anxious for all ethnic groups to live happily, all minorities, all disabled people, in their large forbidding spaces, in their harsh climate."

"But that's a rather positive aspect, don't you find?"

"Good people, nice guys, a little rough around the edges. People really like them, in spite of everything, in the countries they visit. They resemble strange animals coming out of the cold. Polar bears, Atlantic wolffish on their ice floes. Everyone has seen on television our vast, white, silent expanse, the wild animals that suddenly appear in the whiteness of the landscape. I too have seen this, on television. Yet I've never gone farther north than Tadoussac. Some people think that we all live in igloos, in cabins deep in the woods."

"Nothing particularly surprising in that. The folkloric images are always the ones that endure," says Lukas. "They capture the imagination. People associate Spain with flamenco and bullfights, Holland with windmills, France with baguettes and debauchery, Italy with the Mafia."

"Italy, yes. That's why I find the idea of a Canadian swindler selling land in Almuñecar so ludicrous. People think of Canadians rather as an honest, peaceful people, more likely to be dupes than swindlers, always ready to defend the rights of people against any kind of abuse, sexism, racism, the death penalty. An ideal refuge for prisoners escaping from the gas chamber, the electric chair, the firing squad in their native country."

"Are you alluding to Leonard Ming? I was perusing his autobiography in your apartment earlier while waiting for you."

"Yes."

He parks in front of the restaurant.

"I'm amazed you're reading that book," he says. "Amazed that you're interested in that kind of story. Will you explain?"

"I prefer to explain nothing."

We get out of the car. The sea, the sound of crashing, the scent. We find ourselves near the point where the beam from the lighthouse flashes at regular intervals. We notice fishing boats in the open sea.

We enter the restaurant and choose a table near the window.

"It's like being in a boat," I say. "It's like that in my apartment too."

"What do you feel like eating? Fish, paella?"

"Yes, paella, and salad."

"Wine?"

"White."

The waiter comes over to take our order.

"And if I told you that it's truth I'm looking for..."

"Excuse me, but in the plane I heard you mention the child you lost."

"Yes."

"I have three children," he goes on. "They're in Rome with their mother. Two boys and a girl, the youngest. She is thirteen. This may seem strange to you, but I'd like you to meet my wife and children. They'll be here this summer."

"This summer I'll be far away."

"Please don't misunderstand my motives, Éléonore. I don't want to have an affair with you. That's not what I'm looking for."

"And I? Do you have any idea of what I want or don't want?"

"No."

"Maybe I want to have an affair. Maybe that's all I want, a one-night stand or an affair for a week, just a sexual adventure, animalistic, with moans, sighs, secretions, and lots of liquor and smoke."

"I don't think that's what you're looking for."

"Why not?"

"You spoke of truth. Truth is above all that."

"No, truth is not moral, not at all. And what about you, what are you looking for?"

"I already told you: I'm not looking for an affair."

"I know what you don't want. But what *do* you want?"

"To get to know you, quite simply."

"To get to know me, then to sleep with me?"

"Not necessarily."

"Not necessarily, but perhaps?"

"Perhaps."

"To get to know me first?"

"Yes."

"And then introduce me to your wife and children?"

"Why are you attacking me like this?"

"The man I was living with also found me too aggressive. I'm only trying to see things the way they are. Behind the words. Behind good feelings."

"You don't think that someone can want to get to know you, become your friend without having an ulterior motive?"

"I must have translated too many novels."

"I'm not looking for an affair," he repeated. "But I don't dismiss the possibility."

"Of course," I say. "Tonight we will make love together."

"And afterwards, what will we do?"

"Afterwards you'll remember the woman from the plane. I'll remember the man from Almuñecar. To make me dream 'when I am old and grey and full of sleep, and nodding by the fire.'"

I drink some wine.

"The wine is good," I say. "The paella is good. Everything is good. Life is good."

"You say that bitterly."

"Earlier, I met a man on the beach. He claims that Almuñecar is a deathtrap, that people come here to die."

"I'm not coming here to die. Neither are you."

"He claims that everyone here is old."

"In his building, perhaps. In winter there are a lot of retired people who live along the Paseo. But have you gone to the village? Have you gone to the market?"

"Yes."

"Haven't you felt how alive the city is? Haven't you felt its heartbeat?… Tell me about yourself."

"I am a translator, but you know that already. I have translated countless romance novels. Without believing in them. I believed in love, still believe in it, but novels are for dreaming. Not at all the same thing. Another world, outside everything. It's like existing on honey: you become anaemic and sick to your stomach. Personally I dislike honey: I prefer liquor and salt."

"A nice formula."

"Yes, of course it's a formula. When I began to translate romance novels, for a long time I had lost faith, so to speak. I translated other people's dreams to *make* other people dream. But personally, I translated without dreaming. My mind empty. Ironic. I translated countless melodramas without shedding a tear. From one book to the other, I recognized the contrivances, I figured out what was going to happen, and the good feelings ended up making me nauseous. Good feelings, good intentions… hell is paved with them, it seems."

"If you believe in hell."

"It was only the words, the lie of the words that I was stringing together like a robot, almost always the same. Interchangeable. Even the pleasure of finding them, of choosing them in the end lost its charm. I had no more pleasure. It was just easy, an easy way to earn my living, fastidious work. Always feeling that life was somewhere I was not, that I was evolving in lies and impostures. I was floating, a shadow in the fog, moving forward like a blind person."

"I, too, sometimes have that unreal impression of evolving in a no man's land," he says.

"In the novels, the situations repeat themselves infinitely. Perhaps it's this repetitiveness people find reassuring. Only the first names change. Daisy, Wilhelmina, Omar, Esteban, Nadège. These names rotate in orbit, then cross paths somewhere idyllic and fall immediately in love. The authors favour exotic names."

"Lukas?"

"Lukas. Perhaps Éléonore, as well. And the novel could be entitled: *Interlude over the Atlantic*."

"*The Unknown Lady from the Plane*."

"*Off-Season on the Tropical Coast*."

"*Translator of Love*."

"But in these novels, the hero isn't married, because he has to marry the young woman at the end."

"But this is life," he says.

"In the beginning I had fun with it. I didn't have the impression I was working, but playing. In the end it became a conditioned reflex. I could have written the story alone, my eyes closed. On automatic pilot."

"And now?"

"I don't play anymore."

"You opened your eyes?"

"When I was translating, I often felt like slipping non sequiturs into the text. Writing "his flabby thighs" instead of "his firm thighs," talking about the hero's "fairy looks" instead of his "fiery looks." I laughed to myself, imagining the proofreader's reaction. Hoping that she would miss a typo and that the error would be printed, stigmatizing the hero definitively. Writing about the heroine's "soft stomach," "her puny shoulders," "her sagging breasts," "her thighs veined with cellulite." But you see I was a translator for the Love Collection and had to earn my living. The last novel I translated was called *The Farewell Tango*."

"You're pulling my leg."

"No."

The waiter removes our plates, suggests coffee and dessert. I say that I'd rather walk a bit. No coffee? No, no coffee, no dessert. Just the fresh air and the scent of night over the sea.

"I was going around in circles for quite a while," I say, once we are outside. "I decided that the time had come for me to dance this tango. I sent my CV to another publisher, one specializing in best-sellers and true stories. They suggested I translate the autobiography of Leonard Ming, the killer sentenced to die, for whom they had just obtained the translation rights and whose story they wanted to publish as quickly as possible in their True Crimes Collection."

"And you agreed."

"I agreed."

"Why? A bloodbath after immersing yourself in sugar-spun stories?"

"I wanted a change. I was suffocating, stuck in the trap of love stories. I wanted something real."

"A strong sensation?"

"To the heart of my very being. I wanted to leave the lies of love and enter truth."

"The truth of death?"

"Yes."

"Love is no less true than death. Nor is it truer."

"I'm translating an autobiography, not a novel. Leonard Ming is not a character, nor are his victims. I knew, of course, what it was about. I'd read the newspapers. I didn't admit it to myself, but there was something about him that fascinated me. I felt as if the act of killing may have been similar to seeking something ultimate. Ultimate despair."

Lukas takes my hand.

"And now, what do you think?"

"I think I'd like to go home," I say.

"You always want to go home when things get dangerous."

"Where's the danger?"

"You and me."

"You didn't want an affair."

"And you want one."

"Not really."

"I think you're scared of opening yourself up. Why did you insist on entering, as you say, the truth of death?"

"To mourn, probably. As a way of settling a problem with myself."

"Your child?"

"Listen. Because we're speaking of truth, I'll tell you once, just once, very quickly, then you'll never ask me the question again and you'll bring me back home where I'm going to begin working. Here is the truth: I was fourteen when my daughter was born. I wasn't allowed to keep her. She was adopted. I didn't know her. Later, I wanted to find her. I did some research and learned she had died at the age of three. I knew nothing else, I didn't know what she died of, imagined the worst. Sometimes I tried to imagine something gentler, as if death could be gentle. But most of the time, the images that come to me are violent, bloody. That's why I agreed to translate Leonard Ming. Because he kidnapped children, he raped them, tortured, mutilated and hacked them to pieces and threw them in the garbage."

"Stop."

"No, I won't stop. I want to know how someone can do that to a child. I want to understand the executioner. I am translating this book because it's an autobiography, because Leonard Ming killed children and I, his translator, have lost my daughter."

Lukas squeezes my hand. He tries to pull me against him. But compassion, for the moment, is something I can't bear.

Chapter 5

> I do not fear the gangster. I fear his revolver.
> Nijinsky, *Diary*

The sound of the sea has become so familiar that sometimes I don't even hear it anymore. I listen carefully. Yes, she's still there, in front of the house, wailing. Sometimes, she is so calm she seems to crawl; she licks the pebbles on the beach, as if imploring. At other times, she rages, rolls and charges, roars and howls; emitting a sinister screeching as if her large skeleton were going to break off, she vomits and crashes against the rocks.

Leonard Ming loved the ocean when it raged. He liked everything the ocean represents that is unfathomable, pitiless. He liked its power and its indifference. In his autobiography, he compares the roar of the waves to *she-lions*.

During the night, I translated the first chapter. Leonard Ming begins, as it were, with the end. The end of his criminal escapade, the beginning of his escape. He relates the events of June 2, 1985, when he was caught stealing an eighty-dollar vice in a large hardware store in San Andreas. He tells how he spotted the tool, slid it into the inside pocket of his parka, walked calmly out of the establishment, opened the trunk of his car and put in the vice. Raising his head, he noticed the clerk watching him from the doorway of the store and realized his error – wearing a parka in that heat had attracted attention. He escaped on foot. The police were called. His accomplice, Gary Sheldon, stuck to their prearranged plan and covered for him, offering to pay so that the store owners would forget the incident. This was the deal Leonard and Gary had made. Anticipating the worst, Gary kept two cyanide capsules on him. He had always stated he would never be taken alive. Leonard Ming had always stated he would never be taken.

He fled California first by hitchhiking, then by bus, blending in with the travellers, his head held high, then on foot, along the Pacific coast, eating fish that had died and been thrown ashore by the waves, raw mussels, and even, at times, when the hunger became unbearable, seagulls that he managed to trap and stun by hitting them with a rock. He choked back his disgust. Survival: nothing else mattered. "I am a survivor," he repeated to himself. "I am a warrior." Only animals eat raw birds. He knew how to transform himself into an animal. He did not vomit. He was tough, immune to disgust and fear, nerves of steel. His hand never trembled when he killed, he never let himself be swayed. At present, he swallowed anything and survived. He had become the black angel, *ninja*, at whose exploits he'd marvelled as a child. He drew himself up before the foaming waves, as if in competition, swearing at the ocean. "They call you Pacific?" he cried, his voice confronting the tumult. *She-lions*. The only things he could love, if he loved anything at all, were waves and death.

Hunted by a throng of policemen, he did not light a fire, fearing it would give him away. He ate raw whatever he found. In the forest, at night, he constructed a shelter of branches and leaves. At eighteen, he had survived commando training in the marine corps. At eighteen, he had fought in several wars in various parts of the world, knew all about techniques of survival. He was strong, and knew only one law, that of the jungle. He managed to eat, and not be eaten. He identified with the lone wolf, hunting at night, attacking the most vulnerable specimen of the flock. He felt no shame in attacking the weakest. According to his theory, the role of the weakest, their ultimate purpose, is to feed the strongest, this is how nature had decided it. He did not question this concept. He had tattooed on his left biceps a wolf's head with huge fangs. Mythomaniac.

His marine corps training had taught him the essentials: discipline, specialized techniques used in interrogation, how, for example, with one finger planted on the solar plexus, to cause unbearable pain, to cause contortions and convulsions, force people to speak, make someone admit to anything, how to bring even the proudest to their knees. He knew all the strategic points of the body.

His photo had appeared on the front page of the daily newspapers. They called him "The Man from Hong Kong." Once Gary Sheldon was arrested, it was easy to follow the trail to Leonard Ming, to find the bunker, the videos, all the clues. In sensationalist articles, Ming was described as a sadist, a dangerous psychopath, probably armed. He knew this and avoided cities. He wore dirty clothes, stiff with filth and sweat, he ate raw mussels, seagulls, mushrooms, berries. A survivor. He was immune to shame. His face: a mask.

In the back pocket of his jeans, a switchblade. Another strapped to his calf. A revolver in the inside pocket of his parka. He would defend his skin.

He walked north, driven by the hope of finding a boat in Vancouver headed for Asia, of embarking as a sailor, under an assumed identity. He also told himself he could make the crossing secretly, hidden in the bottom of the hold, between the crates and the rats. In his escape, this was his plan, like an obsession. First reach Canada, then head for Asia. Vancouver served as a far-off beacon; he directed all his energy toward the light, repeating the name Vancouver, then Hong Kong, Hong

Kong, like a monotonous melody in his head. Rain or shine, he walked. He had been declared "Public Enemy Number One." He repeated this too, the title became his glory.

He had always wanted to become a man who inspired terror, an enemy of the human race, a total enemy. A menacing entity, a blind force of nature, volcano, earthquake, avalanche, torrent.

He did not think about the murders; his escape absorbed him entirely. He thought about surviving to return to Hong Kong. In his head he saw again the city and its bright signs, and told himself that surely there he could blend into the crowd. He had no other plans.

He crossed the border at night, and at the place indicated by Gary Sheldon, inched his way through the woods, a shadow among the shadows. In the morning, he knew he was in Canada and already less well known. However, he did not relax his vigilance. His hair and beard had grown, but he knew he wasn't unrecognizable.

During the night, I translated this chapter. I didn't ask Lukas up for a nightcap, didn't experience an hour of passionate love with him. I came in alone and went to work at the table with a bottle of mineral water, a glass, cigarettes, the book, the dictionary, my spiral notebook and the blue pen. I turned on the radio. They were playing Chopin. Light piano, melancholic, impulsive. How to read about horrors, translate atrocities while listening to Chopin? It was a waltz, I don't remember which, perhaps *Sentimentale*. Outside, close by, the sea was moaning. Or singing beneath the moonlight? Howling like a wolf? The sea has all these possible voices. I turned off the radio and put on a cassette. Dead Can Dance. On the back cover of the book, I stared at the face of Leonard Ming. Handsome features, to look at him, how could one have realized? These looks were a trap. It had always been easy for him to seduce people, but games of seduction did not interest him. He used his good looks like a weapon. I asked myself: would I have let myself be taken in by the good looks of the devil? Mermaid, your song leads me toward the ocean floor. It was like that from the very start, death and its call. I questioned it. I wanted to get past the lie of its good looks and enter in its truth. Oh! Thanatos, who are you? His face reveals nothing. On the glossy cover, his look remains impenetrable.

He was arrested before reaching Vancouver. For shoplifting. Not a vice in a store this time, but food in a supermarket. Marinated herring, brown beans, cookies, Coca-Cola. Trivialities. What does a killer like Leonard Ming eat? Tiger steaks? Filet of shark? No, he eats brown beans.

He was recognized and spent four years in a Canadian prison before being extradited.

At times, the sea shimmers, she looks like a cradle. You're not wary of her, her foam looks like cream. You want to taste it. From a bird's-eye view, when you look at it you think of the backs of sheep on a blue prairie. Peaceful vision, infinitely reassuring. The coast here is rocky and the water always limpid, washed by its passage on the rocks. Occasionally you see an abandoned object, a plastic bucket, a tricolour balloon the sea is toying with. Because she really is having fun, pushing it out farther, then going out to retrieve it, suddenly propelling herself with unpredictable momentum, turning it over, submerging it, pushing it again. Sometimes she is like that, playful in the sun. The game lasts for hours, the sea relentless, a child on the beach. At other times, she transforms herself into an opaque entity, growling, her foam like drool. Wary of her, you feel the sea is glacial, guess she is implacable. From the cradle she was yesterday, she has become a grave.

When she is rough, fishermen flow into the jetty, tiny shadows against immensity. With broad motions, they throw their lines into the waves. When she is agitated, the fish become more vulnerable, for the sea brings them to the surface. The fishermen throw their catches into plastic buckets that stand beside them, and, attracted by the smell of death, seagulls hover over them, panic-stricken.

When the sky is misty, the sea becomes indescribably opaque, shimmering: metallic, silvery, with luminous sheets here and there that bell out. If not for the imperturbable palm trees that face it, you could believe you were gazing at a skating rink.

The waves speak to me. They resemble songs, romance novels. The same plots with different characters. A big mean fish has eaten a smaller one, a hook has become entangled in a mess of algae. Unluckily for the fisherman, a shortsighted crab has collided with a school of inebriated young shrimp returning from an orgy, two dead, three gravely wounded, a dozen survivors. The front page of the newspapers of Atlantis. Anecdotes of daily life beneath the slack surface. I listen, I sympathize, I smile. Sometimes, the sea is in fine form and tells me old stories – of pirates, mutiny, shipwrecks, and castaways, – stories dating from even before the invention of mythology, spectacular naval battles, the waves entirely red. If you had seen that, she roars, and the sharks, their mouths watering, rushing in for the spoils, you should have heard them howl, these men crying for their mamas at the ultimate moment, it was more moving than a symphony; they always cry for mama, even the most seasoned of them, the most arrogant, the most bloodthirsty of them, and I become this womb for which they long, that will swallow them up. Oh! The young sailors I have lulled, the explorers I've ridden roughshod over. And the cargoes of terrified slaves crammed in the slavedriver's hold, I had no choice but to take them as well. My memory, she says, my memory is too heavy a burden. When she remembers these kinds of things, the sea turns a greenish grey, dark, her waves come up very high, and you understand what the expression "sea horse" means, because the waves really gallop, a savage herd, and you notice, far off, their tousled manes.

When she is serene, she is remembering white sailboats, archipelagos, rustling flocks of albatrosses and pelicans, music and people waltzing on the bridges of ocean liners. The captain sports a white cap, and the women, what perfume, what outfits! Diaphanous, the women, hair in the wind, like pennants, really, proud pennants floating behind the sterns of ships. And the men, she continues, if you had seen the men. I see them, I say. Proud and upright, correct? Yes, proud, upright. Elegant too, in tuxedos, leaning over with their beguiling smiles, their silvery temples shimmering in the moonlight, their immaculate teeth, irreproachable nails, a bracelet around their wrists. They invite young ladies to dance, neglecting their official mistresses, murmuring *honey*, *darling*, to their wives, offering them very dry martinis in which floats an olive, or glasses of champagne. I remember this, she says. There were floating palaces, miraculous catches, there will be again, other dolphins will play with the divers, pearl fishermen, gatherers of coral.

You think everything has been said about the sea, and yet, each time we look at her she is renewed. In the morning, sublime vision, sun rising over the water, a boat heading off or approaching the shore, a cluster of seagulls and their cries. And when the sun sets, the whole setting takes on a pastel hue, pink and blue and tender and muted. The palm trees stand on guard, immobile, then, before you realize it, lampposts are lit, shedding light that adds to the saffron pink of the blurring scenery, slowly replaced by night. The serenity of the moment invades us, we let ourselves go. The sea, so calm you think of fish swimming gracefully, free beneath the gently wrinkling water. But no, we know, beneath the surface, fish devour each other. Gulls fly, then dive. They hunt. A dog, stopping, surveys the scene. If a seagull lets down its guard for one moment, he will pounce on it. A schooner in the distance seems softly lulled. But it sets out its nets. Everything a fight for survival, everything a trap. Cruelty camouflaged beneath the serenity. Yet the dog, the ship, the seagulls are inseparable from the serenity of the moment. When I look at this scene, the feeling of peace it inspires in me mingles with compassion for the cruelty of creation, of which I am a part, compassion for all fragile beings, the predators and those preyed upon.

What is the sea? What is this salt water? What if it were tears, all the tears shed, all those spilled from all eyes since creation, dark eyes and blue eyes, slanted eyes, the large helpless eyes of nearsighted people, protruding eyes, velvet eyes, tears of despair, humiliation, anger, pain, tears of joy and emotion, all tears? What is this sound, this incessant movement, this restlessness of the waves throwing themselves upon the cliffs, then beating against the rocks like exhausted beasts? What if it were sobs, all the sobs of the world, all the despair, all the suffering inflicted and borne since the beginning of time? All the tears gathered together from various places around the world, all the tears rising upon the beach, crashing against the rocks. After all, the tears have to go somewhere, so many flow, the earth cannot drink them all, because then, what would become of the earth, if not a swamp? This way the sea is always full. At night, the moon contemplates it like a large, disenchanted eye.

These thoughts come to me as I walk along the beach. The wind blows angrily today. The sea speaks to me. The nightmare is not over, she tells me. The nightmare will last until the end of time. I look down at my feet: yet jewels sparkle, little pink stones, green, amber, stones white and veined with blue or orange, marbles and fragments of shells that shine when wet, you can make them out between the dull shingles, putrid clumps of algae, fascinating to look at. You bend over to gather one of them, slide it in your pocket. All this beauty, like an offering. Suddenly you doubt having heard right. The dream is so gentle – who speaks of nightmares? I do, the sea answers. She repeats that humanity has not exhausted its reserve of tears. No wave is identical to another, each one is unique and comes only once to the shore, each one has a distinct voice, yet the sea repeats its same old song to infinity. The nightmare, she says, will never cease.

But is the nightmare any more real than the dream of love? Perhaps they are both traps. Have I come closer to the truth now that I am translating Leonard Ming? The fish who devour each other, the fish who are devoured, are they any more real than those who swim freely? And those who lay eggs? And those who breed? Isn't the serenity of the sea an illusion? Isn't her true face one of fury?

Everywhere I go, I see a poster on the wall with a photo of three teenage girls. I saw it this morning at the newspaper stand, then a little later in the window of the bank, then at the café where I stopped. The names are written on it beneath the faces: Antonia Ramirez, Désirée Gonzalez, Miriam Rojas. Two are fifteen, the other, fourteen. Their height and weight are given. Two are smiling, the other, wearing black eyeliner, looks dreamy, her lips parted, her eyes looking vaguely at a point in the distance, focussing on somewhere beyond. It mentions that the evening they disappeared, they were wearing blue jeans, brightly coloured sweaters, jean jackets, sneakers, bags slung over their shoulders. It also mentions that they disappeared on a Friday in November, the 13th, around 9:30 p.m.

Leaving the café, I returned to the newspaper stand, I bought a magazine that tells their story. Then I returned to the café to read it.

The press calls them "las tres niñas de Alcacer." Alcacer is a suburb of Valencia.

They disappeared on the evening of Friday, November 13, around 9:30, heading out to go dancing in a discotheque in a nearby town. An all-points bulletin was issued; the last time they had been seen, they were hitchhiking near a service station, on the way to the road to Picassent. The gas station attendant noticed them getting into a white car.

This news item is the topic of conversation throughout Spain. The press says: good girls, the hypothesis they are runaways should be dismissed, they got along well with their families, in school their conduct was irreproachable, they didn't take drugs. Their teachers and friends confirm this. They earned a bit of pocket money babysitting children in the neighbourhood. People know everything about them: the names of their favourite songs they called up to dedicate on a local radio program for teens. The host still dedicates the songs to them sometimes, in the evening, in a saddened voice, imploring them to come back, or begging their abductors: set them free. People who speak about them call them by their first names; in the case of Antonia, people call her Toni, which is what those close to her affectionately nicknamed her. Calling them by their first names, everyone in Spain feels they know them; they are, so to speak, part of the family. All Spain wants them for their daughters.

I feel a sudden emptiness around me. I am seated at a table, in front of a cup of coffee, living in my own little world. I look at the faces, listen to the silent cries. The cries come through the paper of the poster. Am I the only one to hear them? These faces are howling, their smiles become horribly contorted. Looking at these faces becomes obscene when you hear their cries. A voice worms its way into me: *Voyeur, Eléonore*. My sight blurs and I remain, as if fascinated, my eyes no longer able to break away from the image. I read over the names, passages in the article, I memorize the details, clothing, weight, height, I etch their features in my memory. Antonia has blue eyes, dark hair, bangs that fall beneath her eyebrows. Miriam and Désirée both have long hair, but their foreheads are clear. Désirée has greenish eyes. Miriam has beautiful teeth, white and straight. In the photo, Désirée seems the shyest. Miriam's expression is open, straightforward, and Antonia's is innocent, gentler. Désirée's face is triangular and elongated, and Antonia's rather round. A white car took them away. Where? To what bunker, what prison, what dungeon?

I see them getting into a white car and I wish that car had never travelled along this road, the road to Picassent. I want to see it hit a tree a minute before reaching the service station, see it falling into a ditch, the bloodied heads of its occupants smashing through the windshield, the severed heads of the assassins rolling in the dust. I want the three teenagers to have left fifteen minutes earlier, or later, want them to have gotten into another car, a yellow or a red one, no matter what, or for them to have chosen not to go dancing that evening, but to have stayed at one or another's place listening to records, calling the radio station to have their favourite host dedicate songs to each other.

Images superimpose themselves: myself at the same age, hitchhiking, getting into a white car, then my face crying out from a poster. I see my daughter, the lost child that I invent, just turned fifteen, they are playing her favourite songs on the teen program, she is wearing jeans that cling to her juvenile figure and a brightly coloured sweater featuring perhaps the photo of her idol; they are all like that, she's wearing sneakers, she dances, weightless, she hitchhikes, a white car stops for her, she gets in, smiles, speaks then grimaces with pain and howls, crying, begging.

I leave the café. I walk by the seaside, I ask, "What do you know? For whom are you crying?" I ask and receive no reply.

I walk along the shore, their faces in my head, I try to imagine a life for them. Valencia, city of southern Spain, Mediterranean port, an ancient Muslim kingdom, famous for its oranges. Alcacer, a suburb. I haven't been to Alcacer, but can imagine white houses, patios, fruit trees bordering the avenues, hibiscus and rosebushes. Three figures are moving about. I see the school, the house, the parks, the discotheque. Here are the girls cavorting on the grass, or licking pink ice cream from a cone, or throwing back their shoulders in rhythm as they learn to dance *sevillanas*. And then love, I imagine the first stirrings of love. In secondary school, in the city, all these intrigues, glances cast, obscure language. Who loves whom? They talk about it, interpret, venture hypotheses.

But it's still lies. Just one truth; just one piece of evidence: their faces on the poster. Their crying is also a lie. I'm the one inventing it; I'm inventing an insignificant existence for them, then a horrible end. The only truth is that they have disappeared. The truth is cold and inert like paper.

In Montreal I try to avoid looking at these posters. Frozen like this on paper, the children's looks make my blood run cold.

Leonard Ming also killed children. He raped them and filmed their agony. He sold the films. There are people who love watching children suffer. Exacting customers, who want a guarantee that the blood is real, not ketchup, the screams real. Buyers who don't want acting, but demand the truth of death. Spectators excited by the authenticity of death, finding in this authenticity itself the quintessence of their pleasure. Leonard Ming shot movies for them. Gary Sheldon served as his assistant.

Sometimes he received specific requests. One man, for instance, had mystical fantasies and insisted on flagellation, crowns of thorns, a crucifixion. Another's imagination was inflamed by descriptions of captives bound to a torture post. Scenes of bestiality were, however, in popular demand. Leonard Ming raised two free-tailed bats. He developed a scenario and customers paid him a fortune. Some of them submitted their own scenarios to him. Leonard Ming found the players. But he always played the same role.

At regular intervals, corpses are found floating in the river, in hedges, completely torn apart. They are identified by the remains of their clothing when not naked. When they are in the woods, sometimes vultures have eaten them. They are identified by some small detail, their fillings, when they still have their teeth, old wounds, scars from operations that remain on their corpses, or something else. Their murderers sometimes dug pits, and when they are discovered, their mouths, ears, and eyes are full of earth. When they have remained in water, they are bloated and unrecognizable. But you can still see what they have endured. When they have been tortured, you can't help but see it. You know that their eyes have been gouged out; their nails extracted; a foot or hand severed. You can no longer read expressions of incredulity, terror, or pain on their faces, but you know the agony was prolonged. A forensic specialist notes his conclusions in a report. Trauma, multiple fractures, burns, torn vaginas, and other atrocities. The media pounce on the details, even adding some at times, and they vie with one another to touch the right chords. People read this and shudder. All parents feel a bond. They see the bodies of their children in these corpses, and their children are afraid as well. A wind of terror blows over the cities. If children have heard their parents' comments, terrifying visions haunt their nights. New tears are added to the sea.

Sometimes, though, they never recover the bodies. Then you don't know. People venture hypotheses: perhaps they were burned – a practice often used to get rid of bodies. The assassins load them into the trunk of a car, then take them to an abandoned spot, a clearing, dumping ground, douse them with gasoline and set them on fire. Later, an innocent stroller, a solitary runner, or a couple of lovers seeking a quiet place will fall upon these bones reduced to ashes that will never be identifiable. Or they may have been dismembered and thrown in the garbage. Scavengers sometimes find an arm, a leg, a bloody head emerging from a green bag. It is impossible in certain cases to reconstruct the entire body.

Time passes and the searchers become exhausted. Records are filed away.

But if you read the autobiography of a killer, if per chance you stumble on an account of the trial in the morning newspaper, then you imagine the worst. If you are the mother of one of these missing children, you pray, you beg heaven that the body be found, you want to know, you want to be able to gather at the grave, and at the same time, you are afraid, don't want to know. Your thoughts are confused. When you stop believing that the child is alive, you begin to hope, even though this hope itself is horrible, you begin to hope that the child was only raped, simply raped, not with objects, bottles, sticks, knives. Oh, this hope itself is intolerable, but you cling to it, it's the only hope left! You implore heaven that the child was not tortured, the pretty body not mutilated, this body that you carried and brought into the world, that you cuddled so much, that you fed, washed, clothed, cared for, cradled, that you listened to breathe, this body full of promises, no, you beseech heaven, if heaven has any power, for the body not to have been mutilated. The images that come to us become unbearable. You begin to hope that at least the death was quick, that the killer showed a minimum of humanity. But you doubt the meaning of this word. You hope the killer contented himself with strangling your child. This is what you hope when you've lost all hope.

On the Paseo, I pass mothers holding their children by the hand, fathers carrying theirs on their shoulders. One balances his on a bicycle, a little girl in pink, her arms around his waist. I hear ripples of laughter. Teenagers making a commotion. When I walk in the park, I see grandparents pushing small children on the swings. I see the ones who feed the birds and cats, those watering the flowerbeds, raking the grass. I ask myself: does this make up for that, does the laughter cover the cries, can this love obliterate the hate?

Leonard Ming does not speak of hate. He felt no hate. This kind of feeling was foreign to him because it is still a feeling. Rather, he speaks of what he calls the instinct of the hunter, the exaltation experienced when you track down your prey, then the ecstasy when it is at your mercy, and something else again that he defines as the passion of the researcher. He says that he conducted experiments; the knowledge of pain fascinated him, he wanted to see how far the body could go, the maximal level of pain it could endure, and he states that, in certain cases, the reserves were practically inexhaustible. With Gary Sheldon, he would bet on the resistance of the prisoners. He sometimes lost – some resisted longer than predicted. They had only one breath left and this breath refused to die. The body, constantly renewing itself. In a way, the body fascinated him. He wanted to know which parts were the most sensitive, and which ordeals the most unbearable.

He lingers over the description of Gary Sheldon's erotic fantasies. Sheldon was raised on westerns. He liked the shape and hardness of a revolver, evocative of a man's erect penis. He liked its cold contact, its weight in his hand. Holding it against a temple, inserting it into an anus, putting it in and pulling it out, back and forth, brought him to paroxysms of sensuality. He had created another game: pretending to forget to lock the door of the dungeon. When the prisoner – it had to be a woman – ran into the yard, he would catch her with a lasso. He'd wear his cowboy hat and a checked shirt, his fringed jacket and pointed boots. Women's feet especially excited him. Once the prisoner, bound like a young heifer, was ready for slaughter, he removed her shoes and carefully washed her feet. Leonard Ming would film the ritual. Gary Sheldon would then begin to nibble at her toes, biting harder and harder, biting the ankle, the arch and the heel, sucking on the toes and grunting, finally sliding his sex between the joined bloody feet of the victim and shooting his now pink sperm in her face. Leonard Ming had no such fetishes, but it was he, afterwards, who severed the feet with a mechanical saw. Once, as a joke, because it was Christmas, he wrapped one in paper decorated with reindeer and Christmas trees, tied a red ribbon around it and gave it to Gary. *Merry Christmas, my friend.*

Leonard Ming says that books and films show us courageous people facing death, facing it with dignity. In reality, he concludes, this courage does not exist. Faced with physical pain, they all broke down.

He specifies, however, that facing imminent death, the children proved themselves the least cowardly.

Chapter 6

> I fear lust, because I know what it means. Lust is the death of life.
>
> Nijinsky, *Diary*

On a small street in the village, I found a store selling personalized T-shirts. I was a bit depressed and ordered one in black, with the word *Melancholy* written on it, in white letters. I am wearing it today, in accord with my state of mind.

"Please don't tell me I'm obsessed with morbidity. I'm reading this magazine, I'm looking at this poster, I'm translating this sadistic killer's story, I know it. I'm trying to understand something. I must be on the wrong trail because there is nothing to understand. Nothing to understand about life. You waste your time trying to find meaning."

"I also looked at the photos," Lukas replies. "Me too. I have children. I can't not look at them. I have a thirteen-year-old daughter. I can't ignore them, act as though I've seen nothing, as if I didn't know, as if I were protected."

Lukas has come to join me at the café. He knows all the places I tend to go.

"Last night, I translated the first chapter. The escape from California to British Columbia. But I know that, further on, there will be unbearable passages. I am afraid."

"You could stop, return the book to the publisher. You'll find other work."

"I could, but that would be cowardly."
"Not at all."
"I like finishing what I start."
"At any price? Even if it's a waste of time?"
"Take me somewhere. Take me to your house. Show it to me. When we get there, take me in your arms. I'll let you take me in your arms, and do to me whatever you like."
"Everything I like?"
He smiles.
"Everything."
"I won't hurt you."
"I know," I say. "I don't know."
"Then why do you want to come?"
"I like taking risks."
"You're not risking anything."
"You always risk something."
"You know I'm leaving tomorrow? I'm going back to Rome."
"So, since it's the last time, take me to your place before you leave."

The house stands at the top of a hill, at the exit for Almuñecar. Flanked by two cypress trees, the door opens onto a patio. In the middle, a stone fountain with cherubs. All around, bougainvillea, oleander, geraniums, rose bushes. Just one rose open, salmon-coloured. Wrought iron benches painted white.

He opens the other door and we enter the living room. Empty bookshelves, brown couches, cushiony armchairs; in the dining room a sideboard, a rectangular oak table, eight upholstered chairs. He shows me around: the empty kitchen, empty rooms, beds without sheets, boxes piled on the floor. One room, his, with an unmade bed, rumpled sheets, clothes scattered about, an open suitcase. A fine layer of plaster dust on the furniture. Paintings wrapped in brown paper, placed against the walls.

The terrace juts over the sea. Flowering mimosas, trees bearing lemons, avocados, oranges. Birds singing in the leaves. The sea to infinity, the sea: turquoise at first, then a more intense blue. Sailboats dance in the distance.

"In winter," Lukas informs me, "on a clear day, you can see the coast of Africa."

We sit on the white garden chairs.

"A setting worthy of my Love Collection," I say.

"What would you like to drink?"

"I'd like white wine. And I'm hungry."

"I don't have much to offer you. Olives, tuna in oil, maybe."

"And avocados. Exactly what I'm in the mood for."

He leaves me, then comes back a few minutes later with a tray.

"I emptied the cupboards."

Besides the olives and tuna, he has brought sardines, rusks, honey, and chocolate. He gathers lemons, avocados.

"Not very ripe," he observes.

"They'll be fine."

He pours wine in our glasses.

"I love you very much," he says.

"I could have written this scene in one of the novels of the Love Collection. The setting, the repast. And that line, as well."

"Of course. Anything can be written."

"The heroine would have replied: 'I love you too, Lukas.' To set girls dreaming, or unsatisfied forty-year-olds, disenchanted sixty-year-olds."

"And men?"

"Men don't have the same dreams."

"What would you know about it?"

"Nothing."

"That wasn't really a line."

"And we, alas, are not characters in a novel."
"Alas?"
"I know nothing of you."
"I told you the essential details. I was born in Naples. My family emigrated to Canada..."
"When you were three."
"I lived in Toronto. I studied international law. Now I work in Rome for an agency of the United Nations. I am sure you find this all quite trivial, quite dull."
"You are married, you have three children."
"Laurent, eighteen, Federico, sixteen, and Ophelia, thirteen. There. I had this house built in Spain and came to spend two weeks keeping an eye on things during the final stages."
"Are those really the essential details? Are they what defines you? I want to know things like what you expect from life, if you're afraid of death, how many times you've been in love, if you cheat on your wife, if you had a happy childhood."
"You're asking me too many questions at one time. My head is spinning."
"You can answer them in order or at random. One at a time."
"The game of truth?"
"If you like. But nothing forces you to answer. And nothing forces you to tell the truth."
"I promise to tell you only the truth, the whole truth. I'll begin by the second to last question. Yes, I cheat on my wife from time to time."
"From time to time? Each time the opportunity presents itself?"
"Like many people, I have affairs."
"How many?"
"I'm no Don Juan."
"One-night stands? Or consuming passions?"
"One-night stands. And one passion. Consuming, as you say. To answer the last question, I had a relatively

happy childhood. A normal childhood, if that word really means anything. I wasn't beaten or sexually abused. We didn't live in poverty. My parents got along quite well. In summer, we'd travel to Europe. We were three boys. My father was a small businessman who succeeded and became a big one. He dreamed that his sons would pursue their studies and we did. I have a brother who's a doctor, another works at CBC... From life, I don't expect anything. Life isn't about expecting things... Death, I think about as little as possible. I'm not obsessed with it. Of course, it always pops up in our minds. I don't dwell on these thoughts... I was in love twice before I met my wife. And once after. All in all, I'm a very ordinary man. I have nothing of the hero of the romance novel. And nothing of the horror-film psychopath."

"How do you make love? What do you like? What excites you?"

"Still with your questionnaire?... Beauty excites me."

"What part of the body?"

"The whole body. Its harmony. The voice, the face, the eyes, the hands, the legs, the breasts."

"Big?"

"Not too big. Rather small, but round and firm. With small very dark areolas."

"Leonard Ming tells of how he sliced off a woman's nipple. Ever since I read that, my left breast hurts, continually hurts. Take me to your room. Let's lie down together on your bed..."

The end-of-day sunlight enters through the window. Glimpses of the sea are visible between the branches of the mimosas. The room bathes in pink light. At the same time, the suitcase open on the floor, the white dust on the furniture, and the bare walls give the room a melancholic air that catches in my throat. I restrain myself from bursting into tears.

"They built a bunker next to the house, in Wilseyville, near San Andreas, on Blue Mountain Road," I said.

"They placed ads in newspapers to recruit workers. That's how they got the men. For the women, they used the usual techniques. Call girls, girls taken from bars and discotheques. For the children, too, the usual techniques. Promising to show them puppies in the back of their van parked a little farther on. No child can resist that kind of invitation. At times they themselves replied to ads. Video equipment, a car for sale. They made an appointment, and one evening, at gunpoint, forced an entire family to get into the van – wife, husband, one-year-old baby. Can you imagine raping a one-year-old baby?"

"No. I can't imagine it."

"And yet, it's possible. It's possible to insert an adult penis into a baby's vagina, ram it down her mouth and down her throat, while the mother, bound to a chair, watches. It's possible for a dog to devour a baby beneath the eyes of the mother."

"Stop," he says. "Stop translating this book."

We are standing near the bed, facing each other; he has placed his hand on the nape of my neck.

"I'm obsessing about morbidity."

"I know what you're thinking of," he says. "You're thinking about your baby."

"We were supposed never to talk about it again."

"You think about what could have been inflicted on her. You tell yourself that her adoptive father perhaps placed an ad in a newspaper to sell some sort of equipment, that an appointment was made…"

"I think about it."

"You think maybe it was the sex of her adoptive father that tore your baby's vagina, the mouth of your baby."

"Yes."

"You think of her terrified eyes, you imagine a dog going at her. You want to imagine the worst, that's why you agreed to translate this book."

"I want to go to the end. That's the only way I can grieve. They say that the most unbearable thing, when you lose a loved one, is not being able to see the body. That grieving is impossible as long as you haven't seen the body."

"Yes, that's true, in war, in shipwrecks, in airplane accidents."

"I want you to tie me up."

"No. We're not going to play that kind of game."

"I want to know how it feels to be at someone's mercy. I read it, I write it, but I don't know what it is. I have no real idea of it. I'd like to feel in my whole body, not just my head. We all hide a morbid side within ourselves, something that calls death."

"And something that calls life. I don't want the death within you to call me, for you to call death in me."

"Say mean things to me. Insult me. Spit on me. Treat me like a slut, a piece of garbage, scum, a fat cow, a dirty bitch, a repulsive cunt."

"I don't want to."

"Then say to me: 'My love, I love only you, I've been waiting for you all my life.' Say those lies to me."

He remains silent.

"Say it."

"My love," he says. "I love only you."

"Lies are easier."

"I've been waiting for you all my life."

His hand slides along my back. He pulls me against him. I let go. He takes off my T-shirt.

"Melancholy," he murmurs.

He kneels in front of me, takes off my jeans. He puts his mouth on my sex.

"You are so sweet! So beautiful!"

His forehead rests on my belly. His hands grab my buttocks. I place a leg over his shoulder.

"He said that he wanted to make women into sex slaves."

"Be quiet."

His tongue enters me. Then he straightens up, lifts me, places me on the bed. He undresses in front of me.

"You're handsome, Lukas… Lukas, I like your name."

"It's funny," I say, "how simple physical contact has let us go from calling each other *vous* to using *tu*."

"It's more than simple physical contact."

"What is it?"

"Covering distance. Knowing. Feeling."

"Feeling."

"You prefer *vous*?"

"I prefer distance."

"A border?"

"Everyone in their own domain."

"You're a romantic woman. At the same time, you're not that way at all."

"I am not romantic."

"Earlier, you were asking for ties."

"Ties, me?"

"You wanted me to tie you up. Now you are holding me at a distance."

"You're leaving tomorrow. Distance is already written into this relationship."

"And when I come back, you in turn will be gone."

"We will have had a fling."

"You will have finished translating this book, you will have grieved, overcome your monsters."

I want him to touch me again. I want to be taken, penetrated, nailed. I don't want love, I only want to go through the motions. Spread out beneath this man, pinned to the wall, sitting on his knees. Facing him, his eyes plunging into mine, from behind, my face buried in the pillow. On my knees, on all fours. My ankles wrapped around his throat. Dressed, naked, or just partly undressed, sensitive spots exposed, where the soul throbs and fades away. Yearning to be dazzled, I long for voluptuous death, nothingness. That is all we are, in the end, skin emitting vaguely musky odours, one person's skin sweating against another's, a mouth, lips, hands, banal. A belly button, erect nipples. Thighs clasping hips. Paralysed bones, back pain, smoke-filled lungs, clogged arteries. Body hair mingling together, breath. Oh! To live, what does it mean? Tongues, saliva, teeth knocking together. Eyes closed. Organic fluids. We liquefy, we are only our fluids intermingling, our tears, our sweat, an infinitesimal instant of eternity. We just don't care about emotions. But to live. Below the belt, perhaps, but to climax to the last breath, climax forgetting everything else. Together, we'll explore the lower depths, come on. And for feelings, the nobility of feelings, we'll settle for flamenco. And for moonless evenings, we'll be transported by sweeping operatic arias. Everything stops beating in our hearts. To live elsewhere, as if the end of the world were at hand.

I caress his chest.

"You smell good," he murmurs. "I like your scent. I'd like to carry it away, keep it with me always."

"Speak to me."

"I like your scent. I like your voice. I like your body, your breasts, your hands."

"Ever since I read this book, my left breast hurts continually, that precise point in my body. I'm afraid to translate this passage. The sordid details, the way in which it's told, the spite, the contempt. As if I'd been tortured in another life and my body were remembering the pain."

"In another life, it couldn't have been the same body."

"How to explain then that I remember it so precisely, so acutely?"

"Perhaps it's a collective memory, one shared by humanity. Our collective memory."

"I remember all kinds of pain. As if I had already been mutilated in all these ways."

"When you tell me about this scene," he says, "my left breast hurts also."

"In an essay on death, I read that when suffering becomes too intense, the organism produces a substance whose effect is identical to that of morphine, a substance that paralyses the nerves. Endorphin. Yet I remember the pain. When I see a body being burned at the stake in a film, it's as if my own body were starting to go up in flames. I remember the pain, but death, the instant of death, I've forgotten it."

"The imagination retreats."

"Memory."

"About ten years ago," he says, "I saw my grandfather die. He was unconscious. He had been regularly injected with morphine for a week. What struck me most was the horrible sound of his breathing, something very painful that sounded like a blocked pipe. Exactly what it was, no doubt. When the sound stopped, nothing happened in particular, I mean on his face. His eyes were shut. I didn't feel it was a spiritual event, the soul leaving the body, if you will. No, it was only physical, material, prosaic even, a machine, an engine that stops working."

"What is it that fascinates killers, then? What are they looking for? What fascinates crowds and makes them rush to public executions, congregating at the scene of a tragedy, an accident, a murder? Why did Leonard Ming have customers who bought his films? Who ordered them?"

"You haven't found the answer in his autobiography?"

"I haven't found the answer. I can't find the answer. I am doing all this work for nothing. That's why I wanted to be at your mercy. I wanted to be scared, really scared, to find the answer in myself."

"No," he says. "You would never have asked an assassin to tie you up. In front of a real killer, you would have acted like the others. You would have begged."

"I wanted to beg. I wanted to know how it feels to beg for your life."

"You wanted to act at being scared, act as if you were begging. You knew perfectly well that I wouldn't have mutilated you."

"I couldn't be sure. We can never really know what lies in wait for us. The victims suspected nothing before finding themselves in the bunker and seeing the chains and torture instruments."

"You're like Leonard Ming's customers. You're coming as close as possible to the mystery of death. You want to know the excitement without really being in danger. I could have agreed to act out the role you wanted me to play. But what more would you have learned about death?"

"I'll never know."

"No, you'll never know. Unless you find yourself face to face with a real killer. The role of killer does not suit me, Éléonore. And you cannot please me by playing the victim."

I am silent. Perhaps he is right. My thoughts are confused. It is dark in the room. Darkness everywhere. I am so sleepy all of a sudden.

Chapter 7

> I fear the cold, because cold is death.
> Nijinsky, *Diary*

For cool evenings, I bought thick, grey wool socks and cassette tapes of Spanish music.

Heart and feet warmed. I slip on the socks, huddle under the blanket, and making myself comfortable on the balcony, watch the light fade, the pink invade the scenery, the horizon disappear little by little, then everything gradually become blue night. The beam from the lighthouse shines and the lampposts along the Paseo light up. The breath of life is suspended. I listen to the *sevillanas* and watch the day die. All the seagulls have disappeared. They've gone to sleep, where I don't know. Perfect serenity. A fleeting thought occurs to me: I have survived one more day. I have survived in the scenic splendour, in the mild weather, without hunger or thirst, without pain or cruelty. One of a privileged minority. I want to thank life for giving me this respite.

A shepherd is clamorously leading his goats into the street. He cries: "*¡Adelante! ¡Oh! ¡Cabrillas! ¡Vamos! ¡Vamos!*" and other interjections and grumbling that only the goats have the power to decipher. Over the centuries, man and his beasts have developed a common language. If a car arrives, the shepherd starts running in all directions, whistling and gesticulating, banging his staff on the pavement. The goats then fall obediently into order, unhurriedly, along the sidewalk.

The shepherd wears a wide-brimmed straw hat, carries a staff – I don't know to what era he belongs. Is he directly out of the middle ages, does he live in a cave? The goats, bells around their necks, the delicate tinkling, so joyful, the hammering of their hoofs on the pavement, the occasional bleating. They seem innocent, completely free of malice, and their daily passing fills me with joy. The thought of them being beaten, roasted – even the baby lambs, which it seems are a choice dish in the Granada region – the thought that people eat them makes me sick. Two dogs circle about the flock. The kids are glued to the sides of their mothers. The billy goats are in the middle. A latecomer makes me smile, she always gambols awkwardly a few metres behind the other. Always the same one, a dreamer or a loner. If I were part of the flock, I would be that one, bringing up the back. A few disruptive ones stop for a minute to graze on flowers in the planters that line the buildings. The shepherd whistles, calling them to order. They fall into rank, leaves between their teeth. They always seem to be smiling.

Evening falls; they return to the fold. Always at the same time, they return, obedient and satisfied with their lot, the outing, the few places containing fresh water, the dry grass and the brush the earth concedes to them so meagrely. All together, one movement. They return to the fold, this illusory refuge.

I, however, do nothing but leave. I'm leaving a job. Leaving a city, a country. A man is leaving me. I'm leaving a man without a word of goodbye. And another is leaving me and I'm leaving another. I meet a third, a fourth. I leave a place, leaving no traces behind. Life: an accumulation of moments. I move forward in the sand. The water and wind take care of the remainder. Remainders. Nothing lasts.

The *sevillanas* almost always tell of pathetic love stories. Our eternal love, the singer repeats relentlessly.

Accompanied by castanets and *palmas*. The rhythm is gay; it makes you want to dance. At every holiday, girls dance to these rhythms and lyrics, in their multicolour ruffled dresses, a red carnation pinned in their hair. Clicking their heels, they clap their hands, arch their backs, turn their heads, chins high, shake their hair. It doesn't prevent the song from being unspeakably sad. It was to be expected: eternal love, is there a more mournful theme? It appears that this love was proclaimed before the statue of the Virgin of Rocio, and so? Despite this solemn vow, it lasted no longer than the others. One brief shining moment, as ancient poets used to versify, the ephemeral existence of a rose. A rose we know, nothing is uglier than when it has wilted. I have one on my work table, preening in a glass of water, dawn pink, the first to bloom in Lukas's garden. He gave it to me yesterday morning, before bringing me home. I dread tomorrow, only a vestige of it will remain. It's always like that, eternity, where love is concerned, it's always wilted. Or almost always. Happily, as with any rule, there are exceptions. In novels, operas. Hope lies in wait, tenacious, hope shines through. *Like a pebble in a field.*

I do not yearn for love. I feel neither the desire nor the need to open the shutters, to wallow in nostalgia, to sob, a cushion in my arms, drunk on Malaga wine. Oh my love, you used to be, you were, you. You quivered, yes, there was a time, you and me together, I won't speak of it, I forget, I've already forgotten. Guitars, castanets, *palmas*. Waves rolling in the background on the soundtrack. And the singer has that kind of husky voice that makes me reel, an untrained voice in a village, the aroma of paella wafting, children squawking, horsemen in boleros on their mounts. The words are obvious, always the same, with few variants. You promised me that, and then you left, you left me. What became of our kisses? Our passionate nights, our embraces, our fires, our flames? Our traces in the sand, the contour of our bodies entangled on the rumpled sheets? Oh! These traces, yes, and the shadow of our hands joined, our lips coming together, the ultimate farewell. They repeat it in French too, with other kinds of accompaniment. Piano, synthesizers, violins sometimes. But violins, please no, when the violins begin to play, I... I can bear anything, except the violins. Make them stop, pull out their strings, still their souls so they never make another sound.

This evening the Paseo is calm and deserted. The little old people have gone to bed, others are watching television. I am alone in my building, it's as if I were alone in the world. I am part of the darkness. On the balcony, my shadow has disappeared, swallowed up by the night. Only the *sevillanas* betray my presence.

I stay there a long time. When the music stops, I go in to turn over the cassette and it all begins again. The same words uttered, punctuated by the same rhythms. I lose all sense of time and space.

Sitting like this on the balcony, I look like a convalescent, one of those invalids afflicted with chronic languor or lung disease that they used to send to sanatoriums in the Alps to regain their strength and would wheel out to the terrace facing the snowy summits and place on a chaise longue, a blanket over their knees. By and large, I too am convalescing. My feet rest on a hassock, my legs are enveloped by a blanket, a shawl covers my shoulders. The only thing missing is verbena tea, although I could go prepare some.

I think of Lukas, but banish the thought. Convalescence requires it. We had a fling, we were first names in orbit, our trajectories crossing in winter in an Andalusian town. Nothing eternal. Nothing to write a novel about, or sing a *sevillana* about. At night I turn on the radio. If it's jazz, I listen. I interrupt my work, lie down under the covers and remain still, a hand on my stomach. There is still too much violence inside.

Leonard Ming's violence as well as my own. I remain still, eyes open. I peer into the shadows. I can make out, through the balcony door, the oscillating leaves of the palms. My island beckons. Come, it says. Here you have nothing left to fear. Everything lives in peace, the wolves and the lambs quench their thirst from the same stream. I head for it and turn about. A star flashes on the horizon: the lighthouse at the point. And these lights whose reflection shimmers on the black water: a fishing boat on the open sea. The night is perfectly peaceful.

A voice introduces the various pieces and comments on them. I hear without listening. I like the sound of foreign languages, I like the voices of the night that speak of music in the shadows. The people who host jazz programs have distinctive voices, often husky, at once very serious and very soft. Sometimes it seems as if they have just landed from Venus or Mars. They come spend a few hours with us.

They speak of musicians named Junior, Chuck, or Sonny, and it's as if they are confiding in us. They give dates of festivals and concerts, often implying they were present and that these hours were unforgettable, precious. Occasionally they select pieces recorded in concert, and then you hear the audience applauding in the background. Conscientiously they provide the numbers of the recordings. They do not have radio voices, in fact they don't seem comfortable when they speak, and they hesitate and stammer often. They prefer to listen, you can sense it, but are speaking to those who share their passion, the night listeners. You have the impression that they never sleep, at least never before daybreak. They are the voices of solitary people, who smoke heavily and drink their coffee black, in vast quantities, voices of men with fragile hearts. You imagine them pale and a little hunched over, sometimes shortsighted (and if so they tend to favour dark glasses), dressed with a certain studied negligence, an open shirt collar, for example, wearing crepe-soled shoes, an old tweed jacket with a brown suede elbow patch over a cashmere sweater. Are they wearing a tie? The knot is askew.

Reassuring, these men. They walk with hushed steps in the hallways of the heart.

Jazz is nighttime music; I can conceive of no other time to listen to jazz. Just like flamenco, it tells of despair, of unfaithful women. When it evokes love, it's always plaintive, hopes are dashed, it's always at the moment of breaking up, there's always someone begging the other to stay. It tells of nostalgia, lost childhood, magnolias in bloom. It tells of the South and remembers the hard life, the slaves at work, the cotton fields under a relentless sun. The back lacerated by the whip, improvised gallows at the entry of the estates, all the humiliation, the injustice, they remember. The holds of ships, the voracious rats, the pus-filled wounds, the chains. All this misery it cannot forget: misery is its very soul. At the same time, it has a casual gaiety, impulsively winking and cavorting. It smiles a half smile despite the unfaithful women, years of misery, a big smile showing its gold teeth. It likes anarchy and has no limits. By its obsessiveness, it resembles Arabic rhythms. But mostly it tells of deepest Africa, is full of reminiscences. Very black, yes, it is a music of the night.

I am alone in Spain, it's two o'clock in the morning, my door is locked, the one leading to the balcony open, the sea air enters, pure and cool, iodine-laden, and the jazz carries me away to New Orleans, carries me away to the bars of New York, of Paris. I fly on its wings. Here are the musicians: Sonny bent over the piano keyboard, Junior hugging his contrabass as if it were a mistress he loved madly. Large beads of sweat appear on the drummer. The saxophone player throws back his head. It is dark in the cramped room, a basement no doubt. Jazz does not tolerate harsh lighting. It is created in darkness. I make out their shapes. They are smoking cigarettes, the incandescent tips flying in the half-light, the air thick enough to cut with a knife, ashtrays overflowing. Nonchalant waiters circulate between the tables. The bitter stench of beer and whisky is almost tangible. Certain listeners nod their heads to the rhythm of the music. Jazz possesses them. After each solo, a ripple of applause, exclamations are heard, murmurs of approval. Jubilation. The musicians will take turns and play until the first light of dawn. Men of the night, their music resembles them, inexhaustible.

Sometimes also, with no connection to the setting or the moment, they play Viennese waltzes. How I dance in my lover's arms, how I whirl, how white and diaphanous my dress, how my heart flutters! My lover sweeps me away, away; I'll follow him to the ends of the earth. I let go. My cheek against his shoulder, pressing against the warm silky fabric, he whispers in my ears words similar to those you read about in romance novels: sweetheart, my darling, my soul mate, my love. Deep, his voice, mellifluous, and so firm his embrace. It goes to my head like champagne. Chandeliers sparkle in the ballroom. Outside, a full moon shines down on the garden, the air heady with lilacs. At night, the flowers give off their scent, more intense, heady. Here we are beneath the arbour; in the groves, dresses are rustling, muffled laughter can be made out, confidences are exchanged. Everything encourages love. Still lightheaded from waltzing so much, I put my head on his shoulder. He leans over me, his hand slides through my hair, his lips approach my mouth. His smell is sweet and heady, cologne, tobacco, a touch of sweat.

Other images arise from the music. All of a sudden it's winter, at the sound of this very waltz we skate away together on the frozen pond, my love and I, our cheeks reddened by the wind, our eyes shiny. We are twenty years old. I am wearing a bonnet, and red mittens, a silver fox collar. I smile confidently; life is unfolding, I anticipate the joys to come. So many joys await. We come back in the carriage, bundled in furs, in the snow-filled streets of Saint Petersburg. How innocent, how gay the tinkling of the sleigh bells! At home in the large drawing room we will drink scalding tea from the samovar; a fire will be lit in the fireplace, the red dog will be lying in front of it, the cat and her kittens on a cushion in their basket. The exercise in the fresh air will have whetted our appetites. We will be hungry and thirsty. Our elders looking on indulgently, we will demolish platefuls of goodies, doughnuts and nuts, cherry jam in crystal goblets. My parents will be present, with the aunts, ancient cousins with withered cheeks dusted with talc, wearing grey dresses with lace collars and cuffs, arrayed in the inevitable amethyst brooch. The conversations will be a series of harmless or treacherous gossip. Like in my memories of *War and Peace*. In the afternoon, the girls go skating. Elsewhere, war is brewing, war rages, exhausted soldiers trudge through the snow, horses are worked into the ground, but the girls skate and their suitors are princes they'll marry at the end of the story. Let the imagination waltz. Together, my sweet prince, we will go to the ball and the opera, we will have three children whom we'll name Aliocha, Dimitri, and Danka. We will grow old in our dacha surrounded by elms and poplars, we will grow old not fearing death, we will want to die together, snuffed out at the same moment like soft candles. When I am old, it will be my turn to wear these grey taffeta dresses, these amethyst broaches, I will be invited to tea and will speak harmlessly or treacherously. My grandchildren will call me "Nana," "babushka." Orchard, horses, dogs, innumerable families of multicoloured cats. River trout and pike, small boat rocking, swings under the elms. Christmas trees, Easter eggs hidden in the garden. Bursts of laughter. Imperial court, brocaded uniforms, romantic spot, bygone era.

Yes, the music conjures up images, a host of images. One night in Saint Petersburg, another in Vienna, Paris, Florence, or Prague. Just close your eyes and a world appears. Here are faces, surfacing from my past, ghosts taking shape, shadows moving about in my memory, here are the men I've loved. I have danced with them, swayed in their arms. Here are my lovers, how gracefully they remove their masks. This one has blue eyes, but he's a gypsy with magic hands, that one came from Russia and this other one is limping forward. I liked him so much because of his weakness, I melted then and there. They bow before me, each one offering me his arm, I waltz with each one of them in turn, the dead and the living. With this one, I spent a week in London, made love on the banquette of a night train tearing through the fog. With that one I drank till we were high. Spent crazy nights discussing Dostoevsky, smoking hashish in my room downtown. The characters lived, we were passionately for or against Raskolnikov. They still live: tonight I am dancing with Prince Myshkin, I am dancing with Stavrogin and Dmitri Karamazov. Here is the one who was so jealous, he took himself for Othello; now he is smiling. Here is the bad painter who gave me terrible paintings that I hid in the backs of closets; here is my Jewish lover who was so hairy that, eyes closed, I thought I was caressing an animal. At each love-related depression I remember that I wanted to die. Now the rage has quieted and I dance.

In the still of the night, spread out on the hide-a-bed, I listen to the music, of the radio, of the waves. A hand on my heart, I feel it beat, I feel it calm. The struggle is over. The moon, an eye brimming with indulgence, contemplates the battlefield. Its welcoming brightness alleviates the carnage. The soul rises to it. Humanity filled with goodness, struggling under the weight of its faults, suddenly touched by grace, the compassion of the world.

But if they play contemporary music, concrete music with cries, grating, pounding, I turn it off. Too much violence rumbling inside me that I want to soothe. Too many cries and too much pounding. Too much anguish. My dream is disrupted, the dance is over, or becomes macabre. The ghosts display terror-stricken masks, bloody claws grow from the ends of their fingers. They advance toward me, their demeanour menacing; I see their weapons, chains, daggers, clubs, riding crops; on wheels they sharpen cutlasses. If they light a cigarette it's to burn the tender flesh of a breast, an eyelid.

Added to the music is the howling of victims in the bunker the killer transformed into a torture chamber. The women's voices rise quite high. The killer has a habit of explaining to them in detail what awaits them, the fear he generates intensifying his pleasure. I hear this voice I do not want to hear. I chase it, it resists, reasserts itself. "This morning," says Leonard Ming, "I heard you banging on the door. I don't like that. I'm very angry with you. I'm going to have to punish you. I will remove a nail from your left hand. Because you are right-handed, aren't you? I'm not a brute," he continues in the same monotonous tone, with almost tender intonations. "Your need for your right hand is greater. For the moment, I won't touch it. I will remove the nail of the little finger of your left hand, the least useful one. But in the future, you should be more docile, or else…" He hooks up the video camera, adjusts the lighting, then advances towards his victim, his eyes glittering strangely. The women's voices raise quite high, reach paroxysms, the howling pierces the eardrums. I hear them sobbing, promising: "I won't do it again." "Stop crying," orders the killer. "If you cry, I'll gag you." Yet these cries were music to his ears. He also was aroused by the moaning, he loved the sobs, supplications, the cries of agony. *No kill, no thrill.* These sounds excited him. I know that at times he recorded them and when everything was finished, what was left of the bodies burned or buried, he would replay the cassette and find his pleasure intact.

Outside, a dog barks relentlessly. I don't want to hear it anymore. Well-trained, Leonard Ming's dogs did not bark, but they growled and that was worse. I don't want to think about it anymore. Certain music will awaken unbearable memories in my unconscious. I close the balcony door. The barking is quieter. But the anguish remains.

But if it is Schubert, Bach, or Granados, I listen to it. I listen to this perfection and for an instant death is far away. The hands of the pianist caress the keys of the instrument. Generosity is there, contained in this caress. I tell myself: everything is fine, people live, have lived, looking for perfection, they've lived generously The horror recedes. Leonard Ming does not give me respite for long though. He returns over and over again: "You speak of perfection," he whispers in my ear. "I too was looking for it. Each of my actions was geared toward it. I was a musician, a virtuoso. The body was my instrument, death my theme. I composed variations. No one ever mastered my art like me." His voice troubles me. Did he really write these words, did I really translate them, or am I inventing them? I don't want to hear him anymore. I turn up the volume on the radio.

Tonight they are playing organ music. Funereal music. Strange how music for the dead is peaceful. Respectful of the approach of mystery. Peaceful music for peaceful death. I listen and feel myself relax. Tears well in my eyes, I let them flow. Something within me is freed, unknotted. I feel the drops moving in my tear ducts, which ones will appear first? They pour down my face. Something is freed. Love? Right now I have so much love in me, a meltdown, so much love for the earth and sea, for flowers, goats, cats, children. Everything that is fragile and seeking life, nursing infants in crèches, fledglings pathetically opening their beaks. A wave of love submerges me while I listen to the funereal music, a wave of love for life that will engulf me.

I drift into sleep, I dream. In the dream, there is no more ball, no return by carriage, no children in the orchard whose branches sag under the weight of ripened fruit. In my dream, I am accompanying Leonard Ming in his escape, hiding underground with him in ditches, makeshift shelters. Heat, hard to pinpoint, invades me. Hidden away with him, and our bodies brushing against each other. Inadmissible desire, shameful: it troubles me.

In my dream, there is a little girl who dies. Always the same little girl, never the same death. She is drowned in a bathtub, she is disfigured; I open a cupboard door and find her hanging from the rod. A man approaches her, I can't see his face, only the knife he holds in his hand. It is my daughter; I cannot save her, I've come too late. A little girl is dying and I waken gasping for breath.

An erotic dream is one with death in it. *La mort*, in French. *L'amor*, love in Spanish. I mean *l'amour*, love.

And when you wake up after one of these dreams, you smoke five cigarettes in a row in your bed before being able to get up and go into the kitchen to reheat yesterday's coffee. *L'amour*, I mean *la mort* in the body.

Chapter 8

> I want to write the truth, which is why I lie.
> Nijinsky, *Diary*

The most difficult thing is writing "I." Using the first person, lending my voice to Leonard Ming, finding words in my language to translate his, all involve taking responsibility for a part of his actions. His thinking, I find myself forced to embrace it. I can no longer stay at the surface. I enter into him, our identities merge. There is created between he, dead, and I, living, a terrifying intimacy.

I say I am entering him, but isn't it he, really, who is insinuating himself in me, who little by little, insidiously, is taking over everything? Because even dead he maintains his horrible power, lives on in his words, mine are giving him life. I do not want to yield to the fascination of horror. The same power to destroy, to devastate, he left behind; his words are his imprint and his legacy. He passed like a cataclysm. And I, in the ruins, I count his victims and hobble in the desolation.

I write at night, after the streetlamps have been lit on the Paseo, when the moon traces its path of light along the sea. Alone in the night, alone with the words of death. The moon traces its path, I can make out the glimmers of boats in the distance, shifting reflections, trembling on the black water. The oblivion of the sea, the men on ships, and me with the words. In daytime, I remain glued to my rock. In daytime, on the Paseo, I walk, stop for a cup of coffee, a beer, continue on. When I feel uncommunicative, I buy my cigarettes in the vending machine at the bar next to my place. I insert the coins in the slot, the pack drops down, and the machine thanks me – it can speak. When I feel more agreeable, I buy my fix at the tobacco shop. At the same time I select a lighter with little characters dancing on it. At the café, I exchange platitudes with the waiter about the weather here, the weather in Canada. I exaggerate and he exclaims, raises his hands: "Really that cold?" "Colder still, sometimes, if you take into account the wind chill factor." Life is empty and full. It is filled with platitudes, they are our daily bread. I lend an ear to the conversations, this buzzing surrounding me. Platitudes. Mouths open, lips move; these people too must discuss the weather, reflect upon the food they will order. They scan the menu written in chalk on the little blackboard. Perhaps they have children, grandchildren whose latest escapade they are discussing. Couples sit across from each other, read – he, the newspaper, she, a glossy-covered novel. They have exhausted all topics of conversation. Or perhaps they have no children, no grandchildren, or if they do, don't wish to talk about their escapades. Or perhaps again they are sufficiently comfortable with each other to savour the silence, perhaps the dialogue continues in their heads. When the waiter arrives with their plates, they put down their reading beside them and attack their food. He opens his mouth: will he finally speak to her? No, he gulps down food. Their dialogue must be a soliloquy.

I walk slowly, not really there, an observer of life. Pedestrians brush past me and I hear all kinds of inflections, sounds like music. I hear Spanish and German, English, also languages I don't know, Dutch maybe, or Swedish. I deduce it from the appearance of these people, very blond, and their guttural inflections. Sometimes I hear bits in French, words meaning *Israeli-*

Arab conflict, cost of living, devaluation of the dollar. Philippe resurfaces in my memory, I see him again with his newspaper, his briefcase, hunched over – the weight of the world on his shoulders. *Serbian-Croatian conflict, Bosnia-Herzegovina, peacekeeping, peacekeepers, United Nations.* Then Lukas comes to mind – because he works for the UN. What does he do there? I didn't find out, I was afraid he'd answer that he oversaw peacekeeping, restoring hope in Rwanda.

I think about our actions. The two of us, naked, body and soul, this affair. What was he looking for? True love? *Strangers on a Plane, Coastal Lovers, Eternal Passion*: title for a sentimental novel. *Physical Love, No Exit*: title for an erotic song. *Deep Throat, I Will Enter All Your Orifices*: titles for a pornographic movie. *Orgasm Close to Death*: title for a Leonard Ming film.

Our actions. Nudity, abandonment. A man's sex that I take in my mouth. I think I could bite; with my teeth, I could sever, I could hurt him very badly, force my victim to beg, to cry, to promise. "I'll do anything you want. I'll leave my wife and children. I'll give you all my money." And I, impervious to these promises, could keep on biting, like Gary Sheldon bit women, feel my mouth fill with blood, and while the thick hot blood filled my mouth, feel my sensuality reach its paroxysm. My nails, like a cat's claws, planted on the abdomen of my victim. Orgasm close to death. To the max. *No kill, no thrill.*

I don't think of that when I have a man's sex in my mouth. I don't think of anything, my tongue, my teeth, my nails caress the skin of his chest, my hair touches his thighs and knees, my palms glide over his sides, then I turn over, offer my buttocks to his hands, my hands touch his calves, my hands grip his ankles, my fingers slide between his toes. He doesn't think of that either when he has his sex in my mouth, like the lion tamer, his head in the lion's jaws, his fragile neck between the beast's fangs. He abandons himself, makes himself vulnerable. Pleasure beckons and makes him forget all care, his fragile sex in the teeth of the unknown. *The Vampire's Kiss*, *In the Jaws of the Beast*, *At the Mercy of the Feline*, titles for the "Love Gone Wrong Collection." He isn't thinking of that, but entrusts me with his entirety, his dignity, his life, he trusts me. I do not bite; I have teeth but I glide, caressing him with my hands, my tongue, my hair.

With a stranger, it's easier. That night, I ended up falling asleep in his arms. I woke up a little less sad. Daybreak flooded the room, white and dewy. He caressed my back. I asked him how to say my angel, my wolf, how to say handsome in Italian. *Angelo mio, lupo mio, bello mio.* Vulgar words too, a man's sex, a woman's, how to say them in everyday language in Italian. I repeated them and that excited him to hear me say these words with my accent. In a foreign language, it's always easier. He laughed and called me "Translator of Love," *Traduttrice d'Amore*.

I said: "Right now, I don't want to die. Right now, I'm happy." He answered: "*Non voglio lasciarti*. I don't want to leave you. I don't want to leave you here with Leonard Ming."

He asked me: "Why don't you come to Rome? I don't like to leave you alone here with Leonard Ming and your dark thoughts." I replied: "I'm afraid the words will change. I'm afraid to tell you I'm unhappy with you and for it to be true. I'm afraid to say violent words to you, to say kill me and have you kill me. To say it's the last time, make me a baby and have you make one for me. Make me a baby that I won't keep." He put his hand on my mouth. I was happy and unhappy, wanted to laugh and cry.

Now I am walking slowly along the Paseo and hear passers-by say *Bosnia-Herzegovina*, *Nations Unies*, *United Nations*. They act importantly, even overwhelmed, discussing the state of the world. They have understood everything, no political subtlety has escaped them, they could have been diplomats and directed the future of the planet. They have foreseen all catastrophes. They all seem to think: "If only they had consulted me." They always judge and never make a mistake. They add *Rwanda, former Yugoslavia, devaluation of the ruble, Russian black market*. They have reached retirement age. They own an apartment, a villa on the coast, and are fleeing the rigours of winter in their countries. Wrinkles line their faces, sometimes they are bald or wear thick glasses, are too fat, their stomachs hanging prominently over the belts of their Bermuda shorts, or are too thin, their shoulders collapsing, all these signs of wear, the indignities of time. They walk along the sea without looking at her. *Price wars*, they sigh, raising their arms, nodding their heads, *troop withdrawal, ultimatum*. Some of them walk in small groups, carrying their bags of balls, headed off to play pétanque. Still others, wearing sailor's caps, shake with laughter, jokes I don't understand. Most of them, I'd swear, have never hurt a flea. At least willingly. They are here for the mild climate.

I pass the former bank manager, unhappy in his marriage, and stay a moment to listen to him describe his marital difficulties.

I continue on my way. I go home, turn on the radio. It's time for the news. I make out *bomba* and *Saddam Hussein, Estados Unidos*, but am not sure, am not really listening. Is it this year's news? Or else a retrospective, a retrospective of misfortune... Are they celebrating a gloomy anniversary? I don't know. All news resembles itself.

I take up my translation again. Sixteen years old. Return to Hong Kong. First murder. A little girl kidnapped in a park, raped, strangled. First murder, orgasm more intense than with any other girl. Orgasm approaching death. In a way, by killing, Leonard Ming was testing out his own death. Nijinsky wrote in his diary that the assassin goes to meet his own death.

The facts, chronologically: background in martial arts, arrival in America, arrest for shoplifting, training with the Marines, Vietnam, appearance of Gary Sheldon on the scene, theft of weapons in an arsenal, a year in prison. I translate dispassionately. I want to translate without judging a man's life. I want to understand.

Leonard Ming and Gary Sheldon became friends. They recognized each other at a glance – had the same obsessions. Gary Sheldon frequented the San Francisco underworld, had contacts in the pornography trade. Joint projects were born.

The house. It was a basic cottage in the mountains, in Wilseyville, Calaveras county; it belonged to Gary's ex-father-in-law. Perfectly isolated. They began by filming porn videos. They added chains, whips, the usual accessories, backs, buttocks, lacerated smalls of backs. Animals, children. Their videos found buyers. They earned money easily, mixing business with pleasure.

The bunker. The ads, a macabre joke to recruit manpower. The camouflaged cell, the two-way mirror. Like exemplary artisans, they made most of the instruments.

I know how Leonard Ming found pleasure, how he prolonged and attained it, I know his coldness, his irony, his violence. *No gun, no fun*. I know what he experienced in the face of a beaten body, this mixture of contempt and fascination. I know when and how he began to kill. But I still don't know why. I have only the facts, raw and implacable.

Translating this book, I feel as if I'm living in death. I know everything about the nightmare of death, yet it still remains outside me. I know how to render it interminable and cruel, how to render it ignominious, humiliating, how to invoke it then cast it away, make it pant then yearn, this game. And how to keep alive with death the relationship of lover. I know this too, but know nothing of it, it remains impenetrable. I have only words at my disposal, they reveal none of the mystery.

We don't understand death. We observe phenomena: illness, weakening of faculties, accidents, old age. We observe them with a kind of fatalism. We are not, in a way, even sure we believe in it.

Words terrify us: "AIDS," "meningitis," "gangrene"; some very precise expressions: "to perish in flames," certain expressions, quite vague, "passed away after a long illness." Others are coldly clinical: "drowned in his own secretions," "flesh-eating bacteria." Manifestations of our ephemeral aspect, but even more so, suffering to come, inescapable disintegration of the body at the end of the line. No light at the end of the tunnel. Even more than death itself, than our ephemeral condition, suffering scares us. Because, throughout time, people have discovered remedies for our ephemeral condition.

The vocabulary of death is almost always repulsive. We shrink from it, we pray. "Oh no, my God, spare me!" In these cases, even atheists invoke God. We can't seem to determine if there exists such a thing as a desirable death.

We can, in extreme circumstances, understand that passion itself can be a weapon. Revolver shots fired at the unfaithful, a dagger in the heart, we can understand this type of thing, resign ourselves to it. We call these extenuating circumstances. Suicide also takes on meaning when the meaning of life has been lost. War always seems inevitable, like the atrocities that coexist with it. Once war is over, we analyse the atrocities and declare that humanity was gripped by collective madness. War crimes, extenuating circumstances. For the country, for the flag, a square of coloured fabric flapping in the wind and the rain. The survivors make resolutions, they initial treaties, and we affirm that never, never again can humanity be allowed to indulge in such excesses. Resolutions, worthy feelings. Haggard survivors, streams of tears. Trials are held, a few guilty people executed. When these heads have rolled, humanity breathes more easily. Later, with distance, researchers examine the causes and effects. They write essays that few read. Novelists and filmmakers take over, and their novels are read, their films seen. Their works win prizes; expensive galas are organized to reward the creators. And then another war erupts and everything begins anew, and we understand that in a way, war is an inevitable curse. Bosnia Herzegovina, Rwanda. Sarajevo, Port-au-Prince, Algiers. Tomorrow we will utter again the names of cities and countries. Man is a predator to man. Passers-by walk along the streets of the world murmuring *troop withdrawal*, *United Nations*. Later still, history lets bygones be bygones, assassins become heroes, we erect statues to them.

But for Leonard Ming, how do you find an explanation?

When I translated for the Love Collection, the "I" did not exist. It was always "the young woman" or "she opened wide her cornflower blue eyes." It was always "he took her in his arms." As translator, I was outside, an ironic witness. In the autobiography of the killer, I describe in the first person how he traps one of his victims. I write: "Nancy. Plump. Blonde. Hair dyed probably, but all in all, rather cute. For the videos, it's preferable to have a pretty girl, quite curvaceous. Blondes are popular. Luck was with me that night. No difficulty convincing her to follow me. In the car, she couldn't stop babbling, bombarding me with insignificant chatter. She was twenty-three. A cashier in a supermarket. When she asked me my astrological sign, I replied that I was a Scorpio, even though I'm a Capricorn. She was crazy about the movies. I told her I worked in the video industry and she got all excited."

I get up, pace around the apartment, light a cigarette. I haven't the heart to go on. I know what comes next. I no longer have the strength. What is this truth I thought I would find? I run a hot bath, add orange blossom oil. Pamper my own body. Ease the pain gnawing at my left breast, this sensation of pincers biting into my flesh.

Immersed in hot water, I am surprised to miss the Love Collection and its cloying sentimentality. In *We'll Dance in Rimini*, the fabulously rich Paolo della Rosa organizes a sumptuous reception to welcome Virginia to his villa. The road that leads to the main entrance is strewn with rose petals whose heady scent fills the approaching evening. On Paolo's arm, Virginia climbs the imposing staircase. Would she like to freshen up? A guestroom with bathroom en suite has been prepared for her. Luxury of detail: sprays of lilies in precious vases, taps gleaming, a river of emeralds in a jewel case on the dressing table. "It's too much, Paolo, I can't accept it!" "I insist, Virginia. The emeralds match your eyes perfectly." Like Beauty in the Beast's castle, her heart fills with fear and emotion. In the large illuminated drawing room, the guests await. The windows are wide open on the garden bathed in moonlight; water laps in the basin, wind sighs in the leaves of the sycamores. Well-trained servants serve champagne and canapés. Clinking together, crystal flutes tinkle enchantingly. Outside, crickets chirr, nighthawks call. Paolo offers Virginia a tour of the estate. He explains the family treasures, ancestral paintings, Dresden vases, souvenirs from trips. In the conservatory, Virginia marvels at the abundance of rare plants. He places an orchid in her hair.

Perhaps Nancy read this kind of novel. I imagine her with *Passion in the Tropics* in her purse. I know she had a book in her purse. Leonard Ming mentions this detail – *one of those soppy novels*, he specifies. I've translated so many novels to make girls like her dream.

I get out of the bath. My work table, a glass of Malaga wine, the radio on. Mahler. I write Leonard Ming's "I," but it's Nancy with whom I identify. I have the voice of the assassin, but am the victim, I am blonde and plump, I'm this innocent who thought she'd found love in a bar in the features of Leonard Ming. I have a copy of *Passion in the Tropics* in my purse. Before leaving, I read the passage where Shawn kills the snake with one shot, sucks the blood from Pamela, and carries her, inanimate, to the ranch. Shawn is tall and well built. Leonard Ming is also tall and muscular; when he dances, he sways suggestively. His slanted eyes shine coldly, but what's the difference? Leonard Ming is handsome, has high cheekbones, wears close-fitting jeans, the two top buttons of his shirt are open, his matte complexion looks shiny in the dim light of the bar where I wanted to find love. What difference, if he looks cold? Follow the bear to its lair and tame it. I dance with him. *Crystal Ship* is playing full blast, I drift on a fragile vessel, I dance in the arms of death, I dance in his arms, the sex of death hardens against my stomach. He invites me to his place, I listen to the call of death, and follow him. But what has happened to my instinct of survival? I am like the sailors who succumb to the perfidious singing of mermaids. I follow him, get into his car. But where is he taking me? This mountain road is deserted. The house over there seems so desolate. It is so dark, so dismal here, I want to go home.

Leonard Ming continues: "She really became very nervous when we got to my place. I took her by the arm, and said: 'Do you want to see the house, Nancy?' Once in the bunker she was panic-stricken. Bringing her under control was child's play. I said: 'So you like movies? How fortunate, I have just the role for you.' Her teeth were chattering; she was bound to a chair."

I go out on the balcony and shiver beneath the stars. My teeth are chattering. Will I tie myself to a chair to live the mimicry to its fullest? My right eyelid twitches. I was wrong to read the book before starting to translate it. Like the victims, I know what's in store. I try to immunize myself against fear by working in spurts, injecting myself with horror in small doses.

"I sat across from her, I lit a cigarette," continues Leonard Ming. "I blew the smoke in her face. She closed her eyes. I ordered: 'Look at me, Nancy.' She stared at me, her eyes full of terror. She began to understand. Gary entered. I said: 'Does she appeal to you? Do you want her as a slave?' He spat out: 'You know I don't like fat women. Cellulite disgusts me.' 'So what do we do with her? Should we cut her into pieces? Give her to the dogs? I wonder if they've eaten today.' 'We have an order,' Gary said. 'A customer gets off on mutilation.' 'Another one? They all get off on the same thing.' 'This one, you're going to laugh, gets turned on by the clitoris. He gets off on excision.' 'Look at that bitch,' I said to Gary, showing him the puddle of urine underneath Nancy's chair. 'Now we have to wash her.'"

I write this, the words burning me, I become Nancy bound to the chair, urine running between my thighs, my body stiff with pain; I close my eyes, feel the cold water spray over my sex, my body spread out over a hard surface, I cry out, feel the blade, but don't die, I am Nancy naked and spread-eagled on a wooden table, blood flowing between my legs, chains holding my wrists, my ankles. Death is so long in coming, why does it tarry? The Middle Ages, a dungeon, the grand inquisitor approaches, what is he holding in his hands? I continue to write, I write "I." All the torture, I inflict it, I am at once tormentor and victim, my right eye runs on my cheek, I am this eye, begging and inflicting at the same time, I am this whipped back, this nipple removed with pincers, I am Leonard Ming, it is I who say: "This is the first time I ever fucked a one-eyed woman." I am one-eyed, I closed an eye to write, flesh throbbing, body whimpering, humiliated, dirtied, beaten, bitten, burned and slashed, I implore my executioner to finish me off and I am the executioner, I am Gary Sheldon spitting, I am Leonard Ming ejaculating in Nancy's face and I am that face.

I stop to breathe, but have no more breath. I turn up the radio. Mozart, it's so gentle, this concerto. I go to bed. Instinctively I curl up in the fetal position.

I call upon the memory of a novel in the Love Collection to help me, one in which the hero lights a fire in the hearth to please the young ingénue. The scene crops up in one novel out of two. I translated it, a derisive smile on my lips. More glowing logs, the fragrant smell of maple, the crackling of the flames and the gentle heat. The lovers about to embrace. On the next page, he'll reveal his passion to her, and she'll melt in his arms. I think about these scenes again, and even though I keep playing them over and over in my head, relief does not come. These scenes are all wrong. Truth is contained in Leonard Ming's bunker.

Dungeon, cell, concentration camp, nothing new under the sun. Sacrifices, ritual killings. Public executions, arenas, circus games, crosses and pyres. Gallows, guillotine, wheel, impalement, garrotte, torture post, firing squad, everything has been invented and is perpetuated. I am in the underground of life, in the dark, damp places where murders are committed, in the ugliness of life, amidst the wailing, the abuse and the cries, I am in the tears, the mucus, the excrement, in the cesspool of life, in the stale urine, vomit, sweat, and blood. I am walking in a tunnel leading to hell, colliding against oozing walls, I am in the jungle where everything is a trap, perilous, in the mass grave amidst silence, assaulted by the odour of decomposing flesh. I am among crawling animals, vipers and cockroaches, hideous and evil beasts. "Do you like tarantulas?" asks Leonard Ming. "Look at the pretty tarantulas I've kept for you." I close my remaining eye so as not to see them, but on my body, what's left of it, I feel them creeping. I don't even have a voice left to scream.

Chapter 9

> I cry so as to bother no one.
> Nijinsky, *Diary*

A black dog has adopted me. He is very small, with threadlike paws, and on his face is a white spot in the form of a cloud. I have never been particularly fond of dogs; usually I prefer cats, even the strays, mangy, boastful, blind in one eye, but this dog moves me, frolicking about me, wagging his tail frantically as soon as he notices me. He walks a few steps in front of me, then turns his head and waits for me. If I sit down, he lies down near me. A dog child, overflowing with confidence. I speak to him. I greet him. "So you're here? You came back?" I ask him questions: "Was it you or your mother who was abandoned? How old are you? Where do you come from?" He lifts his eyes toward me and would like to respond.

I bring food to the beach. He follows me to my hiding place among the rocks. He eats anything: bread, tomatoes, cookies. I bring tuna and a can-opener. His happiness is complete. Or else I bring a cheese sandwich and share it with him. He's crazy about honey. He keeps me company. I crinkle up a paper and throw it. He rushes after it. He wags his tail, mouth open, tongue hanging out. He wants to play. I throw the ball of paper in the waves. Together we experiment, an episode from *The Little Prince*: taming, returning at the same hour, gradually coming closer to each other. The little dog is my fox, but it seems as if he's the one who's come down from a star.

He shows infinite patience. I can remain immobile for hours on my rock. He doesn't budge. Against my thigh, he seems gratified, happy in his way. He has found someone. Me too. Since Lukas left, I haven't had anyone, haven't wanted anyone, and now I have this dog. We are in perfect harmony. I walk alongside the sea and he accompanies me. He wants to come on the walk. He never barks.

When I leave the beach, he follows me up to the door of my building. I don't let him come in and he returns I don't know where, not protesting, not insisting. He has the endearing fatalism of abandoned animals searching for a home. In books, orphans are always like that. Becoming someone's child appears to be everyone's goal.

I haven't given him a name. I call him "black dog," quite simply, or "little dog," not even in Spanish.

I tell him not to get attached to me, that it would be better for him to find himself another mother, that I always end up leaving, that I'm not faithful. I say this in my head, looking him in the eye, and have the impression he understands me without nevertheless losing hope. He loves me unconditionally.

If by chance I stop along the way at the grocery store, he waits for me at the door, like other dogs who have a master. He has observed them and knows all the postures. He has this ambition: to become a household pet.

Sometimes I go for a walk in a park in the village, outside his territorial limits. He stops, melancholy, on the Paseo and watches me walk away. He has not adopted me sufficiently to follow me that far. I go to this park at about two in the afternoon, when it is practically deserted. It's a paradise full of rare species, tropical trees with enormous shiny leaves imported from Africa and South America, cacti and flowers, a bird sanctuary.

Today I am here in the park, at the end of the Avenida de Europa. On my way I bought a magazine at the newsstand. On the front page, in red letters: a grandee of Spain has kidnapped a five-year-old girl from a poor area of Seville and photographed her, naked in a bathtub, a rubber duck floating beside her. He declares: "My drug is women... very young." Handcuffed, he follows a policeman down a hallway of the courthouse. His story is told on the following pages. Pedigree going back to the court of Charles Quint, marriage late in life to a famous model, divorce after living together for a few years, various scandals in which he was dishonourably implicated. Orgies with prostitutes of both sexes are mentioned, trafficking in narcotics. I wonder all of a sudden if he wasn't a buyer of live death videos. I examine his face. What do these buyers look like? They are part of an anonymous crowd, those who rushed to public executions, like a show. Perhaps there is an inquisitor among this grandee of Spain's ancestors, who went down to the dungeons to put the question to some suspected witch. I shiver. He does not have the face of the executor, but that of a voyeur. He perhaps began by fondling the little girl. Then, pallid, he would come in jolts, squealing pitifully.

His apparel is described to the last detail: a navy blue jacket, English cut, grey flannel pants, Dior tie with red dots on a silver background, hair impeccably slicked back. No matter how degenerate, it implies, a grandee of Spain always appears dignified. I turn pages that describe other seamy tales. A jealous policeman who stabbed his wife, a baby tortured by two ten-year-old boys, statistics on the ravages of AIDS. Photographs of aristocrats, actresses, sports car racers at winter sports, their pathetic liaisons, their telephone conversations. Among other things, I learn that a princess, according to the Spanish papers, has dubbed her lover *"mi calamarito,"* – my little calamari, my darling. A report on the engagement of the infanta, another on a ventriloquist who got back together with her husband after five months of separation. They pose, hand in hand, on a pink couch. The kitchen section: how to serve spring lamb, ground, braised, flambé, roasted, in stew, in puff pastry. All the parts of its body sacrificed. I skim over all of this, then get up and throw the magazine in the garbage. I sit down again on a bench, look at the slim palm trees, listen to the birds, both concert and cacophony. What are they saying? Their songs are charming to the ear, but we know nothing of what they are saying. Maybe they are gossiping, or shouting abuse at each other. Everything seems so delicate. Do the birds know the torment of the soul? We listen to them without understanding a thing.

An old woman all in black walks with small steps to the garbage and takes the magazine. She sits on a bench across from me, absorbed in her reading. I see her fingers deformed by arthritis, the big violet veins on the back of her hands. I have nothing else to read, have nothing to do, let time pass. She takes a candy from her jacket pocket. I light a cigarette.

We seem to be alone, she and I, in this space, as if in our own little world. Yet no, we are not alone, for all of a sudden I can make out a furtive shadow, one second it's at the entrance to the park, a second later it's slinking between the trees. The shadow approaches. A man in his twenties, with brown hair, dark glasses, blue jeans and a black shirt. The old woman continues perusing the magazine without raising her head. Shadows in parks do not concern her. She reads avidly the report of the misadventures of a Spanish grandee. An idol falls and shatters.

At level with me, the young man stops and asks me for a cigarette. I hold out my pack and lighter to him. When he returns them to me, his cold hand brushes against me. He doesn't say another word, not thank you, nothing. He continues on his way and disappears.

The park seems to have lost nothing of its serenity, yet I am troubled. It is the contact with this damp hand. I like palms to be warm and dry. A new hour passes and nothing else happens. The old woman has not moved. Her old-fashioned purse, imitation black leather with a gold clasp, rests on her knees; she is still reading. I am surrounded by emptiness; it is within me. The birds are napping.

Off-season. In this city I find everything I love: fishermen in the morning pulling in their nets, and their boats that sleep in the daytime on the beach. Small boats anchored that gently sway, and others, with passengers, that sail off into the horizon, escorted by flocks of seagulls with large wings. They are probably coming from Malaga, en route to Almería, Tangier. I repeat the name of these cities to myself: Malaga, Almería, Tangier. That's where, on a boat, I'd like to be coming from, toward where I'd like to sail. Then I would go all the way to Africa and then, still farther south, I'd go lose myself in the Sahara desert... A little farther on, a marina. Sometimes I go there to walk. I sip a cup of coffee in front of the herd of captive yachts and sailboats that sway, powerless, at the end of their chains. I listen to the water lap against their hulls.

I leave the park. When I reach the Paseo, the little dog bounds up, tail waving, ears pointed, looking grateful. Mama is back. He follows close on my heels.

On the way back, I see people in groups drinking aperitifs, sitting on restaurant patios. I see Abelardo, the retired banker, alone at a table. Siesta is over. A crossword puzzle magazine open in front of him, he suddenly feigns interest in this pursuit. He scratches his head, gnaws on a pencil. Above all, he does not wish to seem distraught. He looks it anyway. He has noticed me from afar. I am his last hope, his attentive ear. He gestures to me. Impossible to avoid him. I stop near him, see his distress. Will I agree to join him at his table? I agree, order a cup of black coffee and a Grand Marnier. He starts talking immediately. He shows me the crossword puzzle. Ingenuous smile. His new passion, he explains. Since he retired, he feels the need to keep his mind busy. With his wife, he continues, the situation, already precarious, has deteriorated further. Once more, he has had to flee Madrid. He had just wanted to clarify the situation, talk things over with her. Impossible. She doesn't know how to speak anymore, she only recriminates. And he can't bear shouting. So voices were raised, they'd hurled unthinkable insults at each other. She even said that... But no, he'd rather not repeat it. Vile, degrading insults. I suggest that she must have said more than she meant. No, he interrupts me, she said exactly what she was thinking. This is what they've been reduced to. This is what they've done to love. Love reduced to ashes. And of course the children sided with their mother, he adds bitterly. Ostracized in his own home. A climate of continual hostility. I listen, saying: "*Que tristeza, que lastima,*" I nod my head understandingly. The same old refrain, his story. Like a broken merry-go-round, endlessly revolving. A catastrophic carnival. A moonlit dumping ground. "*Dios mio,*" he sighs. He describes his *estado de alma*, his frame of mind, in affected terms. Several times he looks at me, saying "*disconcertanta,*": I seem confused. This word evidently pleases him; he rolls it around in his mouth. The conversation shifts imperceptibly. He tells me about the heyday under Franco. I learn that, under Franco, Spain had no unemployment, no drugs, no murders, no prostitution. It was a golden age in his country. His head nods gently. The happy era of his youth. I say: "No freedom, either." He protests: no need for freedom when you are happy. What would they have done with freedom? What do they do today with freedom? They drug themselves, kill, indulge in all vices. Before, Franco watched over them. A severe father, but fair and good. Now Spain is an orphan. I finish my coffee and get up. Already? His eyes plead. But I hold out my hand. I must go. Why? I must.

I walk away, the little dog following me. Farther on, I hear the crazy woman scream, because, for a few days, a crazy woman has been haunting the Paseo. She is about forty, obese and ugly. She walks up and down a long sidewalk and cries noisily. She wails in a foreign language, hurling curses, shouting "¡Mama! ¡Mama!" and stamping her foot. She gesticulates and sinks down upon the hard ground. Her despair seems absolute. The first time I heard the clamouring, I thought it was a lost child. It is a forty-year-old lost child, obese and ugly. Passers-by avoid her, children stare at her with slightly wary curiosity. Holding pruning sheers, gardeners continue impassively tending their flowerbeds. Sitting a few steps away on the wall, I observe the scene. Should I go help her? She terrifies me. How can I help her? Too deep, her suffering, almost indecent. Exposed, offered up to people like a heap of bloody flesh. She bangs her head against the pavement, beats her chest with closed fists. After some time, a car stops and a grey-haired woman steps out. She kneels beside the crazy woman, speaks softly to her, caresses her hair. The crazy woman finally consents to get up and follows the woman. The car starts. The serenity of the place recaptured. Blue, sun, flowers, waves. Serenity momentarily threatened. This crazy woman and her cries like a breach, a sudden tear in the scenery. The dark side of landscape. The reverse of appearances. Life, which for a moment gasped for air, once again breathes easily.

Chapter 10

> I like to speak in verse, because I myself am a poem.
> Nijinsky, *Diary*

The bodies of the three *niñas* from Alcacer have been found at the exit of the town of Tous, near Valencia, in a dumping ground where they had been summarily buried. Recent rains having shifted the earth, the hand of one of the victims emerged from the grave. Two apiculturists, on their way to feed their bees, made the horrible discovery earlier this morning. Noticing a belt buckle, one of them began to examine the ground. Earth that had shifted bizarrely caught his attention; he called his companion to come help. They both bent over it and dug a little. A watch appeared, then a hand. They got up, shaking. In tears, they hurried to the station of the *guardia civil*.

It was seventy-five days since the disappearance of the teens had been reported.

The clothed bodies were lying side by side in quasi-fetal position. The cause of death will soon be revealed by the autopsy report. According to the first findings, however, it appears the three girls were tortured. They were each shot in the back of the neck. The funeral will be held Saturday, in their town of birth.

Two individuals are being held for interrogation. A third is on the loose. The two suspects, Enrique Almazor and Miguel Ruiz, were stopped by police barely a few hours after the bodies were discovered. They were at the home of Almazor, in Catarroja, and did not resist the arresting officers. Their rapid capture was made possible by the fact that one of the victims, Miriam, held in her closed fist a scrap of paper with Almazor's name written on it. It was a prescription from the psychiatric hospital in Bétera, where this individual was being treated.

The news hits me like a ton of bricks. I just heard it, on the radio. They interrupted the music program for a few seconds to report it. I was half-listening and it hit me. Those faces I'd seen on the posters, that I'd heard scream. Two men detained, an assassin on the loose. Three bodies curled up in the same grave. Night falls on me. This book I am to translate lies on the table. Leonard Ming, Gary Sheldon, Enrique Almazor, Miguel Ruiz. The names merge, become confused. The words of the book are embodied in them.

Leonard Ming, Gary Sheldon, accomplices, brothers in pleasure. Gary Sheldon kept two cyanide capsules on him. He anticipated the worst. He could not face the idea of being thrown in prison on charges of rape and torture, of murdering children. Ming comments in his autobiography: "Gary was always fatalistic. Even when he smiled, his eyes were sad." A sad killer.

When he found himself at the police station, after the robbery in the large hardware store – once the weapons were discovered in the trunk of his car, the fake licence plates, identification cards and the driver's licences of people reported missing for months, the dried blood stains, brown rather than red, the bullet holes in the door, these traces that, so sure of themselves, they hadn't bothered disguising – when Gary Sheldon found himself at the police station and the interrogation began, he asked them to bring him something to write with and a glass of water. He asked them to remove his handcuffs so that he could write to his wife. He scribbled these few words: *Please forgive me*, and swallowed the capsules, very quickly, with the glass of water. His death, however, was slow: three days in a hospital bed, hooked up to a respirator. But he didn't speak, didn't reveal anything, and Leonard Ming had time to escape. He was on the loose for months, his escape part of his death, and it too was long. I am translating his story. I know his methods, I know how, with Gary Sheldon, he raped and tortured. The scenes come back to me and jog about my memory. The sea, close by, continues her racket.

I break out into a cold sweat.

I heard these words on the radio, uttered by an expressionless voice: *violadas y torturadas*: raped and tortured. Words the news presenters always utter in a neutral tone. They interrupt the music program, give the information, the names, killers and victims mixed together, and the musical program continues. Tonight, an operetta. Soprano voice, rhythmic waltz. *Heure exquise*. The program continues where it left off, the gap closed, death gone back into its shell.

Suddenly I remember the young man in the park, the glacial contact of his hand. I see again the old woman in black sitting on the bench, imitation leather purse on her knees, claw-like fingers turning the pages of the magazine I had thrown in the garbage. An avalanche of images floods past. She, curled up behind a bush, a dislocated arm. A wound to the right temple. Close by, a large stone stained with blood. In the garbage, her open purse. Various objects among the rubbish: keys, a white handkerchief, a comb, photos of children. The wallet is missing. A dark shadow slips between the trees.

Solitude. I feel it like an affliction. All alone here, in this building, at the end of the earth. Lukas had suggested I go to Rome. I want to go to Rome where a man, Lukas, will take care of me. Or else I want to go back to Montreal, take up my former life. Alone here, suddenly I'm afraid of everything, shadows in the parks, posters on the walls, news on the radio, the racket of the sea crashing against the shingles. I'm afraid of the deserted house, afraid of being alone with Leonard Ming and his horror story. Torture, cries, protests, rapes. Afraid of roads strewn with mutilated bodies, afraid of mass graves, dumping grounds on the outskirts of cities where graves were hurriedly dug, green garbage bags containing human remains.

I try to find the sobs within me. Frozen. They don't come. What's holding them back? Why is there such a lump in my throat?

The house is in complete darkness, except for the room I'm in. When I get up, my enormous shadow precedes me on the walls. Suddenly, I'm afraid of the night. I turn off the radio. I'll never listen to it again. But I'm also afraid of the silence. Creaks, hisses that fill the night silence. I go out on the balcony. Isn't that a man's shadow I see creeping along the rocks? Did he just raise his head, noticing the light shining from my place?

I put on my jeans, my wool sweater. I have to find an open space, with people. I run onto the Paseo, alone beneath the streetlamps.

An open bar. I walk in. Standing at the counter, two men are talking. In a corner of the room, a woman is sitting at a table, in front of a small glass of colourless liquor. "*Ramón, otra copa, por favor,*" she orders. Her voice is hoarse, she rolls her r's but not like the Spanish. The owner takes a bottle of vodka out of the refrigerator and walks over to her. "*Gracias, Ramón,*" she says. I sit at the table next to her. She is wearing a white knit dress; pearl necklaces and chains decorate her ample chest; she has rings on her fingers, bracelets on her wrists, and over her shoulders is a long-fringed black shawl printed with multicoloured flowers. Her silver hair hangs down her back in a long braid. She smiles at me: "*¿Francesa? ¿Inglesa? ¿Belga? ¿Americana?*" she asks. "*Canadiense,*" I answer.

"Oh, I can tell from your accent that you come from the French-speaking part," she continues. "From Quebec, right?"

"Yes, I'm from Montreal."

"And may I ask you what a Montrealer is doing in Almuñecar?"

"She's fleeing winter."

"*Ramón, por favor, ¿podría ponerle una vodka a mi amiga de Québec?* Do you like vodka? Come sit next to me, my dear. I'd like to talk to a Quebecer fleeing winter."

"I came here to work," I say, sitting down across from her. "I am translating a book."

"Fleeing winter to come work in Almuñecar. That's unusual. Usually people come here to relax. Is it a book about Spain?"

"No, not about Spain."

She extends her hand across the table.

"I'm Olga," she says.

"I'm Éléonore. Are you Russian?"

"We used to say 'Soviet.' Now we say 'Russian.' The words change."

"But the reality stays the same."

"You think so?"

Ramón brings the bottle of vodka and places a minuscule glass in front of me.

"I am the only Russian of Almuñecar," she continues. They know me in the bars, they keep my vodka cold... *Ramón, por favor, da algo a comer a mi amiga...* I see that you haven't eaten. You are hungry and thirsty, I see it in your eyes. Your eyes are too large. They are haggard. You must drink, you must eat. You should drink frozen vodka while you eat. You are also sad, I can see."

"Yes, I am sad."

"Are you unhappy in love? You're still at that age..."

"They found the bodies of the *niñas de Alcacer*," I say.

"I know. I also heard it on the radio. Ramón always turns on the radio for the news. Drink, drink your vodka, my dear."

Ramón brings us a small plate containing potato salad, another with grilled anchovies.

"You must eat salty food when drinking frozen vodka," Olga continues. "You are too sad. You are translating a book, you say. Is it a nice book?"

"No, it's an ugly book."

"Then you mustn't translate it. You shouldn't burden yourself. I don't understand why people want to read ugly stories. They shouldn't be translated. A nice book could console you."

"The one I'm translating doesn't console me."

"Where do you live, Éléonore?"

"At the Ultima Ola."

"The last wave. I'm not very far from you. I live at Sirenas. You'll come see me. I'll introduce you to my canaries. They sing very well. They sing to music. Each one knows how to recognize a note. I spent years teaching them that. With very pleasing results. I'll give you vodka with caviar and cucumbers and black bread. It's good, you'll see. I have kept certain habits from my youth. Eating habits are the most savagely ingrained."

"Yes," I say. "I'll come. And is a Russian in Spain also fleeing winter?"

"I have nothing against winter. But my life is a story."

"A nice story?"

"There are nice moments. Stories are never exclusively tragic, you know. Even the saddest ones have a few nice moments sprinkled among them, even the one of the girls who were murdered. You want to know mine... what can I tell you? I was a journalist at the time, a foreign correspondent for my country. In France, I fell in love, very much in love... And then, one thing gradually leading to another, because of love, I asked for political asylum, I became a refugee. Went over to the west, which, rightly or wrongly, they call the free world. One day, I stopped being in love with my Frenchman. I came here on holiday and had another affair. With Almuñecar. I didn't want to leave anymore. I know what you feel. For these *niñas*."

"They had their whole lives ahead of them."

"Even at my age, I still have a bit of life ahead of me."

"I am translating the autobiography of a sadistic killer," I say.

"Yes, I know what you are feeling... You are young, you could be my daughter. I never had children. I am old, seventy-two, an alcoholic Russian. It's too late for children. But I see your sadness."

"Tell me about your love affair."

"There is no one love affair, there are twelve, fifty, a hundred. Many men have passed through my life. And women. Children. Dogs, horses, cats, canaries. Each love is a new story. At present you see me, an old alcoholic in Almuñecar, but I had my days of glory."

She expresses herself very slowly, searching for words, with an irresistible accent.

"I am sure you were very seductive."

"I was beautiful. And vivacious. I liked to dance until dawn. Do you dance?"

"Not anymore."

Both customers at the counter leave. Our glasses empty again, Olga motions and Ramón approaches with the bottle.

"*Ramón, mi amiga aqui está muy triste.*"

He looks at me.

"*Y ¿ porque está tan triste ?*"

"*Porque elle piensa demasiado,*" replies Olga.

He pours our drinks.

"*La ultima copa,*" Olga declares. *Sino me voy a emborrachar.*"

"*¿Tu? Nunca. Estas una mujer muy fuerte.*"
"*Menos fuerte que antes, Ramón.*"
He stays a while, bottle in hand.
"*Que piensa en el amor,*" he says, looking at me, "*y olvidará su tristeza.*"
"*El amor es lo más triste que hay.*"
He bursts out laughing.
"*¡Tonterias!*"

Outside: fog and darkness. Olga takes me by the arm.
"I'm holding onto you," she says, "because I drank too much vodka tonight. I'm holding onto your sadness."
We walk along the deserted Paseo, accompanied by the tumult of the invisible sea hidden behind the fog and darkness.
"I'm going to stop drinking," she continues. "Tomorrow, I'm going to stop. I'll to go to a clinic in Benalmadena for treatment, for detox."
"I'm translating the autobiography of Leonard Ming."
"I don't know this man. Here, in a small Andalusian town, at the end of my life, I barely follow the news. I knew, of course, about the teenagers from Alcacer, but killers, their crimes, politicians and their misappropriations of funds, none of that interests me anymore. I have left these things behind me."
"He came from Hong Kong," I say. "He killed about thirty people, children, women, men. He tortured them."
"We had Stalin. You know the names as well as I do: Hitler, Pinochet, Duvalier and the others. I have already read their story. I don't want any more of it. Tomorrow I'm going to start treatment. My health is going down the drain."
"Before leaving Montreal, I saw a Russian film that made me cry for weeks. *Burnt by the Sun.*"

"I don't watch movies anymore. The sea is my spectacle from now on. I watch from my patio and it's the most beautiful film. It changes endlessly. One day, an action film with waves rushing in. The next day, a romantic film, then a poetic film, another day, a war movie. It's never the same and it's still the sea."

"The sea speaks to me."

"It speaks to all of us."

"What it tells me is sad."

"What it says depends on the ear of the listener. To me, it only tells happy stories."

"I like everything Russian. Before I left, I also read Nijinsky's *Diary*."

"Ah! Nijinsky! I'm old, but still too young to have seen him dance. *The Afternoon of a Faun*, right? What a pretty name for a dance!"

"He went mad."

"Mad? Are you sure? They always say that about people who have a different perception of life. I doubt that they are. But it's probably reassuring to believe."

Suddenly a car appears, its headlights like two large pink eyes peering through the fog, then it disappears.

"Why do you insist upon translating this story?" she asks me. "There are other books."

"I thought that this story was truer than the others."

"For true stories all you have to do is read the newspapers. Personally I don't read them anymore. I like books to take me away, make me discover other worlds. At present, I only read poets. I'm reading Alfred de Musset and Pushkin, Rilke. Authors you can't go wrong with, as you can see. Immortals. You have to translate beautiful books. You have to translate poets."

We stop in front of the Sirenas.

"Do you want to sleep over?" she suggests. "I think you are afraid to go home alone."

"I am afraid. But I'll go home alone."

"Thank you for your arm, sad young woman."

"Thank you for comforting me."
She kisses me on both cheeks.
"I like the way you are," I say. "One day, I'd like to live here, like you. I like you with your shawl, your jewellery, your vodka, your canaries. And your love stories. I would like to be like you. I hope to see you again."

"Seeing me again is easy. I don't sleep much anymore. At my age sleep is a waste of time. In the daytime, you'll see me on my patio, you'll hear my canaries sing. And at night, if you look for me, you'll always find me in one bar or another."

"And your cure?"

The trace of a sardonic smile.

"Tomorrow," she says.

Chapter 11

> I'm afraid of death, which is why I don't want it.
> Nijinsky, *Diary*

Today, it's raining on the sea.

When I woke up this morning, there was no more horizon. The sky and sea had merged, a pale entity. Fog enshrouded the landscape, there was no more landscape. We were elsewhere, as if in nothingness. For a few very brief moments, the sun pierced through the clouds and a luminous path wavered over the grey water. Then it started to rain.

Very dreary rain, gentle and dreary. No wind. Nothing, no one. Only rain over the sea.

On my balcony, I am sheltered. I settle down with a glass of white wine. From the first loge, I contemplate the spectacle, this liquid universe. Everything merged. Even the green of the palm trees has taken on a greyish tinge. It looks as if everything is on the point of disappearing.

There is no wind, just plain rain. Even so, a few brave souls are out running, nothing can stop them. They stay in shape no matter what the weather. Others take small, hurried steps beneath their umbrellas.

I don't go out to feed the black dog. I have no more black dog, I lost him yesterday. He was frolicking around as usual on the beach when I arrived. A blond giant had gotten there before me. A kind of Viking dressed in old cracked leather, his long mane tied behind his neck with a shoelace. When he saw me, he asked me in halting Spanish to whom the dog belonged. I thought about it, then answered that he belonged to no one. I could have said that I loved the black dog, but this love was our secret, and so I said nothing. The man bent down on the rocks to call the dog, who hesitated between him and me. Then the giant took him in his arms and carried him away. I heard him speak kindly to the dog in a foreign language. His old rusted car, falling apart, was parked right near the Paseo. He got in with the dog and they left. I stayed there, dispossessed.

I threw the cookies I had brought with me to the seagulls.

I repeated to myself: there, it's done, now I'm alone in the world, absolutely alone, that's what I wanted. I thought that I could have told the Viking I didn't belong to anyone either and that perhaps he would have invited me to get into his rusted car. He would have carried me in his arms and placed me in the front seat, with no luggage, no past, no book to translate. Later, he would have fed me and murmured reassuring words in a foreign language. We could have taken the dog with us and formed a family. We would have continued travelling across the roads of Europe and, in a year, we would have had a real child.

And now, it's raining. Bodies have been dug up, a dog and a man have gone off, I remain on my balcony, waiting for I don't know what. Tomorrow, I could return to the beach and meet another dog, a lost cat, a man ready to adopt me. Or else I could never move again, dry myself out under the sun, then disintegrate. Everything is possible and nothing is possible. I could stop translating this book that repels me, stay here, drink chilled vodka, eat cucumbers with Olga and, when I run out of money, go cavort on the beach while waiting for a Viking to come take me away.

I find no answer. I stay there. Slowness of life. I say, for example: today, I shave my legs, tomorrow, I'll sweep the house. Those are my only plans. The day after tomorrow, I'll go change money at the bank, and the following day I'll wash my hair. Another day, I'll go to the market and buy vegetables to make ratatouille. I'll buy them, but will leave them in the salad bowl on the table. I'll say: tomorrow I'll cook them. I'll gaze at these colours, the violet of the eggplant, the green of the zucchini, the red of the peppers and tomatoes. Another day, I'll go eat grilled fish, seasoned with garlic and thyme, at one of the restaurants on the beach. Every night, I'll translate. At the end of the week, I'll have translated sixty pages. The following week will be the same. Sixty more pages and so on, until the end. Then, the corrections. Wash my dress, hang it on the clothesline, take in down in the evening, all clean and sweet-smelling, burying my face in it to intoxicate myself with the scent of the wind.

I obey no one, have no schedule. I go entire days without speaking to anyone. I listen to the execrable voice of Leonard Ming and that of the sea. I would like to translate as if it were nothing, only a mundane job, stringing words on a page without worrying about their emotional power. Not a translator of love, but of words, like a machine.

In Montreal my neighbour, in summer, would pull out the hair on her legs with depilatory forceps, sitting placidly in the stairwell. She would explain: "I'm passing the time." I want to pass the time like her. One by one, the words, the men, the glasses of vodka. I'd spend time placidly. The poster with the children's faces, the girls, their confident smiles, dreamy, their eyes serious or laughing, I wouldn't see them, bent over my brown legs, scrutinizing the skin in search of an undesirable hair. I wouldn't adopt stray dogs. Like Olga, I'll have given up on newspapers and movies, and will settle for just one spectacle, always the same, just one truth, always and never the same. The sea beneath the rain, grey, the sea beneath the sun, turquoise and blue, the sea at twilight, pink, the sea at night, black. In bars, they'll keep my favourite liquor cold. I'll walk in, my head held high, I'll leave tottering. I'll have become an alcoholic, but people won't judge me. I'll have vague plans to go for treatment, I'll talk about it without believing in it, like a good joke. People will smile. People will say the name of Leonard Ming to me and I'll answer that I'm not familiar with this man. I'll go home in the fog, on the arm of sadness. I'll be a hundred years old, with no more illusions or disillusions. The works of poets will be my bedside reading. I'll read Baudelaire. I'll read Verlaine's *Sagesse*. I'll have no memory.

I could stop translating this book, stop being dragged down by it. Only translate poetry that no one will read, but what's the difference because by translating it I'll be bringing it to life again? Adding to the beauty of the world rather than to its ugliness.

Today, it's raining on the sea. I don't go out, I remain shut in like a prisoner in the bunker in Wilseyville. Wilseyville. This name, however, isn't evocative of California. When I think of California, names beginning with San or Santa, Los or Las come to mind. Wilseyville is more reminiscent of New England. Wilseyville could also be a city in Canada, in the far north or far west, a city in rainy England.

Leonard Ming tells how Gary Sheldon convinced his father-in-law to let him have the cottage. One Thanksgiving Day, the whole family gathered around the table; traditional meal, roast turkey, squash and corn bread. Leonard Ming was not present, Leonard Ming wasn't part of the family. He was serving time in prison when this family meal took place. But a video attests to the family celebration. Gary played it often, proud to show how, by arguing, he reached his goals. In the video, you can see him become impassioned when he talks about the threat of nuclear war, of the necessity of having a shelter. He could have been an evangelist had he not been a murderer.

Try as I may, I can't picture Gary Sheldon celebrating Thanksgiving, carving up the turkey, stuffing his face with cornbread and mashed potatoes. The image of him with a knife in hand, however, is quite plausible. But it's difficult to imagine a killer among his kin. All killers have families. Leonard Ming speaks very little of his. Father in Hong Kong with his brothers, his mother gone back to live in Yorkshire after the divorce, one sister in Ontario, another in Alberta. Nephews and nieces, no doubt, whom he doesn't mention and who one day will say: "My uncle was called Leonard Ming." Or who won't say it.

Gary Sheldon had a brother, Donald, whom he detested. Gary had a wife, Connie, whom he met at the Marin County medieval fair. She, in a white dress, a crown of flowers in her hair, he, wearing a small green hat with a feather, taking himself for Robin Hood. He photographed curious onlookers who posed next to his goat. Called Sir Lancelot, this goat was transformed into a unicorn, a fake horn in the middle of its forehead. Gary often looked at the photo album, and the photos stored in a shoebox: the unicorn, Connie, the flowers, their wedding in a small San Francisco church, Lonnie Gunnar, the witness, nicknamed "Fatso," five feet eight inches, four hundred and twenty pounds; the motel, in Philo, where Sheldon had worked as a manager for a year. Videos of Connie, naked, in a corset, in a black brassiere, in nylons and garter belts, satin, silk, leather, sex, breasts, buttocks, feet. Connie masturbating herself, Connie on all fours like a household pet, Connie with her legs spread, tied to the bed. In one video in particular, Leonard Ming is screwing her while jabbing a knife into the mattress, a few millimetres from her head.

Close-up of Connie's wild-eyed expression. Games. Souvenir photos to warm the heart on melancholic evenings.

Leonard Ming tells how they began like that, they began with Connie in a motel in Philo. They had got the idea of making movies, then the idea of selling them. Then all they had to do was find the players.

They needed material, so they got the idea of the classified ads. They needed a van, so they got the idea of taking Lonnie Gunnar's. Exit Fatso. They needed a second car. They got the idea of getting hold of Donald's. Exit Donald Sheldon. They needed manpower and got the idea of having slaves work for them. Then they got the idea of sex slaves.

One thing gradually leading to another.

Today, it's raining on the sea. I'm not going out. Someone is ringing the doorbell. I don't answer. Perhaps it's the banker bringing me an umbrella. He always wants to bring me something in the hope that I'll listen to him repeat his boring story. Or maybe it's Lukas who's come back. Perhaps it's the Viking who's looking for a dog, a dog who's looking for a mother, a wet cat. Or else a murderer who'll ask me for a cigarette.

Chapter 12

> I don't know what to say. I don't know what to silence.
>
> Nijinsky, *Diary*

Here are the facts: on Friday, November 13 of last year, the three teenagers, of their own free will, got into a car, a white Opel Corsa. The car was driven by Miguel Ruiz, twenty-three years old, called *El Rubio*, the Blond, whom the girls vaguely knew. Miguel Ruiz was in the company of Antonio Almazor, twenty-six, a repeat offender well known to police. According to Ruiz's deposition, the girls agreed to go have a drink with them. The two men then took them to a deserted shack that they called the *Porqueriza*, the piggery, which served as a refuge for Antonio Almazor, escaped since last March from model prison in Valencia where he was serving time for forcible confinement, rape, and assault.

Once there, Almazor forced Antonia and Désirée, at gunpoint, to get out with him while Ruiz raped Miriam in the car. After sodomizing her, Ruiz kicked Miriam out of the car, then, grabbing her by the hair, dragged her to the shack.

It appears that a third individual, still unidentified, was already at the scene. Noticing her two friends, naked, bloody, faces swollen, lying on the garbage-strewn ground, Miriam began to scream. Almazor punched her in the face, then twisted her arm brutally. Very brutally. You could hear it snap. Miriam's arm hung, inert.

The three girls cried and begged, but their torturers were too excited to stop. They swore not to report them. There was, however, absolutely no reason to trust them. They were finished off with a bullet in the back of the neck.

The massacre over, the three accomplices dressed their victims. They took clothing at random, giving Miriam Désirée's sweater, Désirée Antonia's jacket, Antonia Miriam's panties. They loaded the bodies in the trunk of the white Opel, and stopped at Almazor's home to get a blanket. Once there, they asked Antonio's brother, Enrique, to help them bury the bodies. The feeble-minded Enrique, nicknamed Elvis because he could never be separated from his guitar, agreed to go with them. Taking a shovel, they headed off towards a dumping ground at the exit for Tous. They intended to dig a deep grave, but the earth was rocky and they were unable to dig deeper than a metre. They then decided to enlarge the grave and place the corpses down sideways.

According to the autopsy report, the bodies showed contusions and multiple fractures to the face, chest, spine, pelvis, as well as wounds to the vagina and the anus. Désirée's left breast had been mutilated. All three adolescents had broken teeth.

At the scene of the crime, they found empty cans of food, a brassiere, a bottle of wine, a vial of an aphrodisiac elixir, used needles.

Here are more details. Neura Almazor, from São Paulo, Brazil, the mother of Enrique and Antonio, works slitting the throats of chickens in a Valencia slaughterhouse. She and her nine children live on her meagre salary, crowded into a dirty, dilapidated dwelling cluttered with assorted refuse, where a brand-new television occupies the place of honour. Neura Almazor has undergone three abortions, a hysterectomy last year, and at forty, her face is prematurely lined with wrinkles, her back hunched over, and her hands misshapen with arthritis. She met her husband Fernando in São Paulo at the age of fourteen. She fell madly in love with him because "he was a sensational dancer." A violent alcoholic, he died three years ago from cirrhosis of the liver. Four of her sons were imprisoned several times for various misdemeanours: drug trafficking, car theft, exhibitionism, forcible confinement of a minor, assault and battery, counterfeiting and forgery, resisting a law enforcement officer in the performance of his duties. In Antonio's room were found pornographic magazines, newspaper clippings showing ladies underwear, a sex manual. One of his brothers, Victor, age thirteen, declared to the press that they'd never find Antonio because he was as "agile as a panther."

Enrique was undergoing treatment at the psychiatric hospital in Bétera. In his mother's words, he is "sick in the head" and never approached a girl because he is too shy. He has, however, already spent a night in prison, having undressed and masturbated in the public square. He suffers from incontinence and one day was discovered frying his own excrement in a pan.

On the front page of *El Pais*, the seven brothers, including a four-year-old whose face is dirty, pose, looking dazed, in front of their hovel. In the photo inset, Neura is shedding a tear.

As for Miguel Ruiz, he is the son of a retired military officer. Left motherless at a very young age, he was placed, along with his sister Encarna, in the Valencia orphanage, which he left when he turned eighteen to work as caretaker in a piggery. Imprisoned a few times for trafficking narcotics and possessing stolen goods, he found work as a truck driver, which he kept for a few months before again finding himself unemployed. In the interview the father gave to El Pais, he declared he would not survive this shame and that the until-then honourable name of Ruiz was forever tarnished.

Leonard Ming explains nothing. Just the gestures, the precision of the gestures, just the words, the cries for help, the supplications, the verbal abuse and the scenes of massacre. His memory is infallible. But never any explanation. Is it heredity, his childhood, the humiliation he'd suffered, the beatings? I don't enter into him: I don't penetrate the secret. At one point, he writes: "I am a wolf, that's the only explanation. I am a predator, the taste for blood was imparted to me with life. I am a wolf: the sheep and their shepherds had better watch out." Further on, he explains his philosophy of life in these terms: "Haven't people, throughout eternity," he asks, "admired the elegance of the panther when it pounces on the gazelle? Is there not grandeur in the falcon as he swoops down on his prey? Don't people prefer tigers to stupid sheep, and cats to rats? Haven't these symbols of power always served as models? And what about those Americans, who condemn me today with horrified expressions, isn't their emblem the eagle? Aren't the cars they like called Cougar, Barracuda? We, human predators, following the example of wild animals and birds of prey, are indispensable to the immutable balance of life," he concludes.

He also points out that executioners have existed in every time period and throughout the world. He had read a great many books on the ways of carrying out death in ancient China, in decadent Rome, in the Second World War concentration camps. In his autobiography he dwells on these torments and their sophisticated variations, explaining that he had resolved to experiment with everything and go even further. In most religions, human sacrifice was common practice: didn't they offer virgins to the Minotaur and the Sun God, didn't they light pyres to burn witches? And the public has always relished the sight of torture. His argument is based on this: cruelty may also be considered and practised as an art form. Just open a newspaper, no matter which one, to measure how much people crave this kind of exquisite pleasure. Leonard Ming asks the question: how to explain that so many people still read the works of the Marquis de Sade? Just look at the success of horror films and pornographic magazines, he adds, the craze for chains, whips, handcuffs and other accessories. His videos, he says, gave male and female viewers their most intense orgasms. Seeing him operate, certain women became ecstatic. And he was convinced that his autobiography would become a best-seller, be translated into all languages. Death, cruel death, is a powerful aphrodisiac.

Fortified by his experience, he also claims the following: the tortured body reaches unsuspected climax.

Miriam, Désirée, Antonia. A Friday the thirteenth in a shack called the Piggery. Kicks to the face, broken teeth, dislocated spines, chests burned by cigarette butts, torn vaginas, all three girls covered with drool, blood, urine, sperm. Unsuspected orgasm.

This morning I found a letter from Lukas in my mailbox. He wrote me this:

Dear Translator of Love,

I don't know whether to call you "tu" or "vous." Since I'm unsure, I'll use "vous."

I told you I was an ordinary man, without any horrible memories. It was a lie, because I do have such a memory: hidden very deeply within me. Since we met, it has stayed with me, haunting me. I know that I owe you the truth, you who seek it so relentlessly.

I was sixteen. It was a summer evening, in the middle of a heatwave, in a Toronto park. It was one of my first experiences with alcohol. A gang of us guys had bought bottles of cheap wine. A girl was there, one of us came on to her on the street, she followed us.

I didn't touch this girl. I did not rape her. Through my alcoholic haze, however, I saw them pull off her clothes, saw her struggle, saw her limbs pinned to the ground, heard the smothered screams, the grunting.

I left at the same time as the others. We left her there, lying in the grass, her torn clothing scattered around her.

I wonder if anyone knew her name. Personally, I never did.

I wrote that this memory was buried deep within me. That isn't true. It has never been very far. This incident left me with a feeling of shame that will never leave me. Like an indelible stain on my conscience.

I wanted you to know the truth about me, even if we are never to see each other again.

Lukas

The power went out. The entire village is plunged into darkness. And I have never seen so many stars. Lying on the couch, I contemplate them. Innumerable, how they shine, how perfectly serene the night! The letter is on the table, near Leonard Ming's book, and the newspaper, *El Pais*. I stay, eyes open in the serene night. Here, nothing harmful, everything sleeps beneath the stars. But elsewhere in the world, bunkers, dumping grounds, shacks, piggeries, slaughterhouses, people slitting the throats of chickens, killers as agile as panthers, predators for whom the taste for blood came at the same time as life itself. Elsewhere in the world, mothers waiting anxiously by the phone for news of their missing child. Elsewhere in the world, nests are pillaged, hares hunted down, gazelles expire caught between the claws of wildcats. The immutable balance of life. Elsewhere, mass graves, battlefields, settlements bombarded, processions of refugees carrying their scrawny babies, their belongings, women with scarves over their heads, their eyes haggard, their disjointed remarks about the news on television; in the background the still-smoking ruins of what was their house, their village, their past; on the soundtrack the cries of famished children and their mothers who have no more milk; the camera pans its objective eye to the puddles of muddy water, the devastated harvest, the immobile bodies in grotesque poses. A microphone in hand, foreign correspondents gather comments from unkempt survivors, question dignitaries and the military. Humanitarian convoys set out. Humanitarian. I think about the ambivalence of this word. Always new gaps to fill, new hungers to appease, new wounds to tend. Other survivors appear onscreen to attract the world's attention. They have turbans on their heads, women are covered in *chadors*, they wear tattered T-shirts on which you can still recognize the Coca-Cola logo, the head of Sylvester, of Charlie Brown, their hair is frizzy, ragged children follow close behind in small groups and wave their hands in front of the camera; in the background, soldiers wearing helmets in battle dress, tanks; on the soundtrack gunshots, the rattle of machine guns, the silence of death, the silence of life facing death, the roaring of life facing death. And then, trains full of refugees leaving stations; images from archives, in black and white, where other convoys leave from, en route to Treblinka, Auschwitz; current images of tubs, cockleshells on the water, their cargoes of prisoners like cargoes of slaves in olden times, tossed about by the waves, pushed by adverse winds, their cargoes of prisoners crowded on the bridges like cargoes of slaves in the past crowded in the holds, heading for the same America. America, this same Eldorado, the eternal mirage.

It is they who should be asked their opinion on the immutable balance of life, of the unsuspected climax elicited by suffering.

But here the night is perfectly serene. The sky resembles a garden. Never have I seen so many stars. The cool contact of the sheets against my legs fills me with pleasure. I wrap my arms around a pillow; its cool downy contact against my cheek reassures me.

Leonard Ming was right: his book became a best-seller. Already more than a million copies sold. Fourteen countries have requested and obtained the translation rights. In Hollywood, talk of making a movie. The name of a prestigious star for the lead role whispered.

And I, translator of love, paid ten cents a word by a publisher to translate this story, treating myself to a trip to Spain. In the end, am I so different from Leonard Ming and his clients? There is still blood, still money at the end of the trail of blood. I am a part of the same system.

A discordant sound suddenly breaks the harmony of the serene night. An alarm has sounded. Someone must have approached a car, attempted to steal it.

I close my eyes, but the noise persists for a long time in the deserted night. The moment I drift off to sleep, I hear it again resonating like a fog horn, a call or a cry.

Chapter 13

> I am life, which is why I want to live.
> Nijinsky, *Diary*

Sunday, day of celebration. The city comes to life. Families from the surrounding area come to picnic on the beach. Folding tables, chaises longues, blankets, parasols, spots of colour on the grey shingles. Some have lit fires in a steel barrel, placed a large frying pan on it. They are heating up paella, whose fragrance fills the air. You'd think you were at a village celebration. Furtively, lovers. I see them slip away, hand in hand. Little girls roller skate confidently on the sidewalks. Riders on their mounts return to the mountain, dressed up as hidalgos, with black hats and boleros over their white shirts with puffed sleeves. The horses stamp and snort. On the back of the sea, it looks as if sheep are frolicking.

Weeks have passed since I arrived here. A new season has settled in, and with it, people on vacation. The wind no longer blows with the same violence. In the park at twilight, brass bands are rehearsing for the Holy Week processions. I have finished my translation, I feel light. I reread it to correct the style, the spelling mistakes. It's only a book, a story. It isn't mine. I correct the form.

The three teenagers from Alcacer were buried, and other stories have come to the forefront of the news. A Spanish fishing trawler seized off the coast of Newfoundland. Spain sent a ship from its armada to the rescue. Armies confront each other, diplomats negotiate.

The word "Canada" recurs on everyone's lips, uttered with anger, indignation. Caricatures depict it as the features of an obese one-eyed pirate with a wooden leg, measuring the mesh of a fishing net.

I correct the style. Because, of course, there is the style. Mission accomplished. Salary earned. Killer dead and buried. Book sold in all good bookstores.

Friday, at the market, I bought lavender. I put some in all the drawers, and when I open them, its tender scent drifts up to my nostrils. I keep opening them, just for this satisfaction. I also bought basil because it's good with the tomatoes and the eggplant. I went food shopping, I filled the cupboards and the fridge. I don't want to feel like a transient anymore in this house. I bought curaçao and Malaga wine, I bought rice, pasta and rusks, goat cheese and sheep's milk cheese, packets of soup. I want to be able to withstand a siege. I want to be able to shut myself in here for a month without hunger obliging me to go out. I bought butter, coffee and litres of UHT milk, eggs, cream, peas, and oranges. I filled the freezer with frozen pizzas and lasagna. My cupboards are chock-full. Contemplating all this food, I experience a new feeling of security. I bought almonds and cashews, mandarin oranges, strawberries, lemons, grapes. I want to be able to crave anything at all and for it to be there, at arm's reach. I bought cartons of cigarettes, bath salts in various scents, PH balance shampoo, suntan lotion. I bought sweet almond oil and candles. I want life to be good and lavish me with its riches. I want life to show its generosity. I enter the bedroom, I open the drawers, I breathe in the fragrance of lavender. I walk to the bathroom, open the medicine cabinet, look at the bottles, read the labels, moisturizer, lotion for smoother skin, toner, cleanser, face scrub, anti-age, anti-wrinkle, fluid, cream, lotion, emulsion, balm. All these words are good for me. I read the directions: massage gently, rub in completely, rinse thoroughly. I go to the kitchen, open the cupboards, look at the cans of food, the jars, honey, apricot jam, the packets, packages wrapped in cellophane, jasmine tea in a metal box. I open the refrigerator, look at the fruits and vegetables in the bin, the butter in its compartment, the milk and the wine on their shelf.

I slice the eggplant, drizzle it with olive oil, sprinkle with thyme, garlic, and basil and put it in the oven. I macerate the strawberries in curaçao. In a stemmed glass, I pour the Malaga wine that is so heady. I go out on the balcony, look at the hibiscus below in the garden, such humble flowers. The sea ripples before me, a limpid blue, spots of foam seem to cavort on the backs of the waves. I raise my eyes: the sky is also blue, a blue so intense and pure that I call it "Mediterranean." This is what life gives me. This is how life is when it shows its generosity. Like a mother breastfeeding, like a rich and charitable man untying his purse strings and distributing gold pieces to the destitute. It gives everything. It gives milk and salt, it gives water and fruit. It fills the senses. To the eye, it gives beauty, trees, rivers, birds, gardens. To the ear it offers music. It gives unsparingly, it squanders.

I have four cups but always use the same one, always the same plate too, as if I had adopted them. After drinking coffee, I rinse out my cup and leave it on the drainboard, ready for the next. As if I didn't dare take everything that life gives me, all the cups, all the plates, all the loves. Life is generous and I skimp. It extends its largesse and I cry over death.

Today, I want everything. I break two eggs into a bowl, prepare an omelette for myself and put it on a plate, the eggplant on another, bread on a third. A tablecloth – it's a day of celebration – I put the plates on it. In a vase, carnations. A carafe of water, a bottle of rosé wine, fruit in the salad bowl. I washed my hair, am wearing my long dress, my earrings, and my shawl.

On the beach, a little girl plays with a white dog, her mother prepares the paella, her father and her two brothers fish with rod and reel, and I eat in front of the spectacle of the sea.

Then I go out, drawn by the hum of celebration. Manolo is working in the garden. I always see him puttering about, a toolbox open beside him, or watering the grass, absorbed by some humble and necessary task. I like men who work the earth, who repair things; I like their rough hands, the black nails. The men who repair or water have slow gestures, as if they had all of life in front of them.

He greets me with a slight nod. I approach him, I talk to him of hibiscus, the parasites that eat away at it, pitiful sight, wells drying up, of the yellow cat basking in the sun. He tells me that there hasn't been enough rain, that the seawater has infiltrated the ground water. I look at his hands and feel his look linger on me. Moment of restorative warmth. Sometimes, he tells me anecdotes of Spain's past. He speaks of the last sultan, Boabdil, who, when chased from Granada by the Catholic Kings, cried while casting a last glance on the beloved city, and of his mother who had said: "Now, cry like a child for what you did not know how to keep like a man." On the road to Granada, a place called Supero del Moro, the sigh of the Maur, commemorates this event. He tells me the story of a marquis who lived in Cazulas, very close to here, in the last century, an evil man named Don Paco Castro, who galloped in the fields with a servant attached to his saddle by a rope. Seeing him pass, workers would raise their arms, muttering "¡Hijo de puta! ¡Hijo de puta!" and he, believing it was a mark of respect, puffed himself up, saying to his servant, "You see how the people love me? You see how they greet me when I pass?" One night he was ambushed and the villagers shot him with a rifle whose bullet went directly into his heart. When the police assembled the villagers to find out the name of the perpetrators, all the men rose at once. I like when Manolo tells me these anecdotes and ancient Spain comes back to life. Today, he asks me if I like a song he names, one I don't know. He can't remember some of the words and it's irritating him. He adds that it often plays on the radio, that I must have heard it. He hums the tune for me. I don't know it. I say that no, I'm sorry, I only listen to my cassettes, or else to classical music. When I tell him that he sings well, he laughs and shakes his head. I tell him: "At present, our governments are at war over turbot." He looks dismayed and shrugs his shoulders. "It's only politics," he replies.

I cross the Paseo. I walk along the seaside. I arrive at my hiding place, my refuge in the rocks. Lukas is there. I'm not really surprised. He gets up as he notices me.

"I knew that you'd end up coming," he says. "I would have waited until tomorrow, until the day after. I couldn't accept the idea of never seeing you again."

"Now it's *tu*?"

"Now it's you."

"It's me?"

"After the letter, I couldn't get used to the idea of your receiving it, reading it, and saying to yourself, 'I spent a night with this man.'"

"I spent many more with Leonard Ming. But I read your letter."

"I won't try to justify myself. I don't want to say it was a youthful indiscretion."

"No."

"It *was* a youthful indiscretion, but that doesn't justify anything."

"No."

"I still want to make love to you."

"I also thought of you, I thought of that night. I have finished my translation. I translated at night, every night."

"At night I thought of you, all alone with death."
"They found the bodies of the three teenagers from Alcacer."
"I know."
"Raped and tortured. A grave dug hurriedly in a dumping ground. The bodies thrown in."
"I know."
"A bullet in the nape of the neck, the way a rabid beast is killed. They cut off Miriam's left breast."
I approach him.
"Put your hands on me. Take me in your arms."
I take the hand he places on my shoulder, run it over my cheek, kiss his warm, dry palm.
"I often think of men's hands," I say. "I think of their gentleness. I think of their strength."
He takes my hand, kisses my palm.
"Women's hands soothe. I like women's hands, so nimble, so strong and so fragile."
I kiss his neck. My hands cross at the nape of his neck.
"Men's necks. They're solid. They hold up their heads full of concepts and dreams."
He places his lips on my hair.
"Women's hair intoxicates. I like women's hair, these ties so strong and fragile."
I unbutton his shirt, place my hands on his shoulders.
"Men's shoulders. When I think of men, it's their shoulders that come to mind, broad and strong and hard."
He kisses my eyelids.
"Women's eyes. They resemble the sea, enigmatic and changing. They contain all tears, all joy and all promises."
I run my face over his chest.
"Men's torsos, I like to rest my head on them. Men's torsos reassure me, strong and silky. Men's torsos, that hold their hearts."

He takes off my dress. He takes my breasts in his hands.

"Women's breasts. They are generosity itself. They give milk and sensuality."

I unbuckle his jeans; I pull down the zipper. I run my hands over his buttocks.

"Men's buttocks, I find them... how shall I say... I find them provocative. So small, so muscular. Sometimes almost inexistent."

He kneels down in front of me. He presses his face against my stomach.

"Women's stomachs. Like a pillow for the head. Women's stomachs hold all the secrets. They are like life."

We lie down on the sand. I remove his jeans. I caress his thighs.

"Men's thighs. They make me think of trees, straight and solid."

His hands run down my sides, rest on my hips.

"Women's hips. Nothing is more beautiful than women's hips, wide and full."

He takes my arms and draws me up to his face.

"Women's mouths. Soft warm lips. Smiles like honey."

We remain intertwined. I caress his arms.

"Men's arms. Their biceps, I like to feel them, hard spheres beneath my fingers."

His hands reach down to my buttocks.

"Women's buttocks. Round like full moons. Women's buttocks, so sensual."

I place my mouth on one of his nipples, then the other.

"Men's breasts. Touching. Like the memory of their lost femininity."

"Women's voices. I like women's voices, at once serious and soft. Women's voices caress the ear."

"I like men's voices. I like to hear them when they get impassioned about an idea. I like those voices, at night, on the radio, that introduce jazz programs. I like to hear men laugh and sing flamenco."

I lift myself up, lean on an elbow, look at him for a long time.

"I like men's bodies. Their long limbs, the hair on their chests."

He straightens up, takes me in his arms, lays me on my back, places his head on my stomach, caresses my legs.

"Women's legs are all the harmony in the world."

His hands move slowly up my body. He raises his head, takes a breast in his mouth, caresses the other with his thumb. My fingers run over his spine. He lies down on his back. I place my head on his stomach. I caress his legs.

"Men's legs. I like men's legs, slim and solid, planted firmly on the ground. Men's feet, bony and pale, that always seem too big."

I take his sex in my hand, rub it against my cheek.

"I like a man's sex. I like it when it is hard and full of life."

His hand runs over my back, his fingers enter me.

"A woman's sex, warm and wet and fragrant. Like a mysterious cave. You slide against its walls. You never finish exploring."

I take his sex in my mouth, take it to the back of my throat. I caress it with my tongue, my teeth.

"Women's mouths," he murmurs. "So warm, so soft."

His finger massages my clitoris, he brings me to the verge of orgasm. Then I mount him, straddling him, my hair in his face, my hands on his shoulders. I feel him enter me, entering the very depth of my being.

He turns me over on my back. My legs wrap around his waist, my arms around his neck. His tongue is in my ear. On me, his breath, his sweat. His sex in me comes and goes, enters and withdraws, then enters, then withdraws again, enters again.

I come in waves, like the sea.

"I came here to find death and found life. You are my life. How do you say 'you are my life' in Italian?"

"*Sei la mia vita.*"

"*Lukas, sei la mia vita.*"

In his arms I anticipate his absence and, in his arms, happy, my body suffers, anticipating his absence. In his arms, fulfilled, I have a foretaste of the emptiness and, happy, cannot prevent myself from suffering. I say that I have found life and that I want to die.

"How do you say, 'I want to die' in Italian?"

"You always speak of death. Forget death."

I take his face in my hands. With my thumbs, I caress his eyelids, I follow the contour of his nose, his cheekbones, his lips. I hold his face between my palms. My gestures have a gentleness that overwhelms him.

"How do you say 'I am happy' in Italian?"

"*Sono felice.*"

"I am happy with you. *Sono felice.* Our time is limited. But I take this love as a gift of life."

Chapter 14

> I cry, because I love life.
> Nijinsky, *Diary*

Lukas has gone back to Rome. We didn't make plans to meet. Life, chance will decide. And now that I've finished my translation, I'm setting myself some deadlines. I know that I need to go back and give the publisher my translation. I could throw it in the sea, burn it on the shoreline, wipe out this story. That won't stop it from having happened.

I tell myself: when my little jar of night cream is empty, I'll go. Or else I put on lipstick and tell myself that I'll leave when the tube's used up. When my shoes wear out, when my supplies run out.

It's true, everything I love is here, all that evokes life and sensuality. Munificent life. Death too. Whether I stay or leave, there will always be life, there will always be death. Whatever the city, there will always be dumping grounds. And even if I were to translate all the romance novels in the world, killers would still come to write their stories with the blood of children. But, in spite of the bloodshed, in spite of the rumblings of war, children will be born who will be loved, men and women will still embrace before the sea, like flowers growing on a mass grave.

Now I hear clamouring and the tinkling of bells. The shepherd is passing by, with his goats.

Almuñecar, January 1993 – April 1995

*This book
set in Stone Serif 11 on 13
was printed
in October 2001
at Imprimerie Gauvin,
Hull (Québec).*